Happy Reac

Nigel Messenger is a hotelier who was inspired to write his first novel, *The Miracle of Michmash*, having heard about an extraordinary battle in the Old Testament which was mirrored in a WW1 battle in Palestine.

He has been working with the Poppy Factory for almost 30 years, supporting wounded, injured and sick veterans into employment in the UK.

He is now writing his fourth novel, which also has a WW1 theme.

Nigel N. N. Messenger

October 2019

This book is dedicated to all those who defend our shores.

Nigel Messenger

FROM EDEN TO BABYLON

AUSTIN MACAULEY PUBLISHERS™

LONDON • CAMBRIDGE • NEW YORK • SHARJAH

A CIP catalogue record for this title is available from the British Library.

ISBN 9781528912013 (Paperback)
ISBN 9781528912020 (Hardback)
ISBN 9781528959971 (ePub e-book)

www.austinmacauley.com

First Published (2019)
Austin Macauley Publishers Ltd
25 Canada Square
Canary Wharf
London
E14 5LQ

To family members, past and present. To Amicia and Herbert, my grandparents; and Uncle Eddie, who all frame this story.

To Amicia's granddaughter, also called Amicia, who generously allowed me to use her excellent school project on the life of her grandparents. Amicia and her family live in Texas and are great supporters.

To Tom Adam, who does extremely valuable work for the Poppy Factory and generously allowed me to use very moving letters written by his relative Daniel Cunnington in WW1.

To my family, too many to mention, who have supported me in so many ways; and to my long-suffering wife, Maura.

Table of Contents

From Basra to Simla: Herbert's Rescue Mission

With home-bred hordes the hillsides teem,
Troopships bring us one by one,
Vast expense of time and steam,
To slay Afridis where they run.
The "captives of our bow and spear"
Are cheap, alas! as we are dear.

Rudyard Kipling

I recognised Eddie Manwaring-White as soon as I saw him in Basra, even though the left half of his face was blown away. His emaciated frame gave witness to the terrible suffering he had endured for so long. The poorly tied bandage had fallen away from his face revealing a horrible open gash which had festered with maggots but there was no evidence of gangrene yet. His left eye was partially exposed, and his mouth was torn into an evil grin. His left nostril was torn away. I could see that he had suffered appalling wounds, pain, starvation and subsequent neglect. I thought he was dead at first: he lay still and had a grey pallor and if he was not dead yet, he very soon would be. I had first met him in Ladysmith, Africa, when he had saved my reputation, career and possibly, my life.

Earlier, I had watched as the river steamer loomed into view down the Shatt al-Arab River towing a barge towards the rudimentary docks at Basra. The wounded should have been transported on the hospital steamer but there were just too many men being carried from the horrors of Kut five hundred miles away. But even these steamers were now little better than the barges, with terrible overcrowding, filth and were ridden with disease. The rain was drizzling miserably as I stood there waiting for the barge to pull up at the concrete platform. I saw dozens of coils of ropes hanging over and running along the sides. I soon realised that these were not ropes at all but lines of excrement which had solidified and clung to the sides of the barge. As the boat came closer, I could see a cloud of mosquitoes and flies above the open deck which housed hundreds of our wounded men. The haze of miasma and the toxic, disgusting smell soon enveloped us. I quickly inserted two bits of cotton into my nostrils and tied a smock across my mouth and this helped a little, but I was still close to throwing up. Even my stoic Sikh havildar (sergeant) flinched but managed to keep his composure.

We watched as the Arab crew safely secured the craft to the pier. Havildar Singh stepped on board and turned his head away in horror. He never showed his emotions, so I was surprised to see his temporary loss of control. I followed and cried out in shock. I had never witnessed anything like this before and I had seen enough terrible sights. The wrecked British bodies in Africa and the vile inhumanity of our concentration camps had, I thought, made me immune from all human excesses—but I was wrong. This was much worse. There was shit and blood everywhere attracting millions of flies and mosquitoes. There were hundreds of brown and white bodies exposed to all the extreme elements this horrible country could inflict on them. The men were lying side by side pressed together to maximise space. I cried out in disgust and shouted to the Arab boy I thought was in charge.

"Hey, you! What the fucking hell is this? What kind of bloody bastard are you? I'll have you horse-whipped. Explain yourself, you vile piece of shit."

For those who know me, this kind of language was unheard of, in fact, I had never spoken those words before but of course, I had heard them often enough and worse. My havildar showed his shock but not his surprise. My shouting made no impression on the crewman and he turned his back as if he did not understand or even hear me. I decided to put in a formal complaint to the dock master; in fact, to add this to a long list I had already made.

That's when I saw Eddie; I recognised him immediately despite his terrible wounds. The men lying alongside him had a horrible range of wounds and diseases: limbs were missing, stomachs torn and exposed, and even gunshot wounds in hands and feet, evidence of self-injury to escape their hellhole. One man had a suspected broken hip and was lying in an awkward curve. He must have suffered terrible pain. There were cases of malaria, typhoid, dysentery and even one case of measles.

I spoke to my havildar to ask him and his men to take some water to the living and to remove the dead. We had a cart nearby to carry the bodies away. We would bury them in the cemetery and very carefully record their identities and gather their personal belongings, if they had any, for their families. I suspected that many had been robbed of their possessions. As usual, Singh had anticipated my wishes and his men were already attending to the afflicted. This was not unusual as we had fought, worked and played together for almost twenty years in dozens of campaigns, beginning with the Boer War. I turned again to Eddie and looked at his poor face. I swear I saw a slight flutter of his left eyelid and I knelt to feel his neck for a pulse. First, nothing at all and then I felt a very faint flicker. I whispered into his ear and brought out my water bottle, opened it and let a few drops fall onto his lips: initially, there was no reaction and then an imperceptible movement of his lips and tongue. I was very happy he was drinking and with the right care, he had a very small chance of staying alive. It took nearly twenty minutes to slake his thirst. It was the least I could do in return for what he had done for me.

Havildar Singh and his men had started to carry the men by stretchers to our steamer at the other end of the harbour and to find them comfortable quarters. He arranged for the doctors and nurses on board to come and help in this huge and challenging task. Basra is a dirty infested port, so it was important to get our men out of there as quickly as possible. I was told we could take men to the General Hospital in Basra, but I had heard the conditions there were not good. There were reports that it was overrun by rats. No, I would take them back with me. In addition, this whole place was shambles. Who the hell was in charge round here? We had queued for days to get a mooring and then we were told that unloading would take six weeks. Six weeks, I ask you. What kind of organisation is that? I would have had the man shot in India (well, probably not but I was very angry indeed!). There were not even any cranes to assist unloading. This was a scandal.

13

Havildar Singh came to tell me that all the men were on board and resting as comfortably as possible. We had plenty of Indian medical orderlies to look after them. He had buried fifty-three bodies and the remaining one hundred and seventy-one men had berths on board. I decided that we were full enough and we would get these men back to India with all haste and keep them as comfortable as possible. There was a queue of steamers waiting to dock to look after the men from several other barges and hospital steamers which were now approaching.

The poor treatment of our wounded had become an international scandal. It was my job to bring the steamer into Basra to collect the sick and injured and to take them back to Bombay and then by trains up to the hills in the north where the air was fresh and cool. We had a large hospital on standby in Simla. At the same time, the availability and distribution of essential supplies had been inadequate to put it mildly and so we were fully loaded with food, medical supplies, rope, tents, tools, weapons—just about anything an army on the move needs. We even brought in horses and mules and we needed special quarters and care for these precious animals: other items including medicines and medical supplies, clothing and boots, tents, food and a vast range of weapons and we prayed these would be dispatched with haste, but we had our doubts. The supply up till now had been poor and even with our efforts it was still extremely inadequate. My job was to deliver all these supplies to the port of Basra and thereafter, they would be the responsibility of others, although having met some of the ongoing logistics team in Basra, they filled me with little confidence, but it was not in my remit to ensure delivery to the men on the front line.

The whole organisation of the port was disgraceful, and it was a filthy uncared-for place. I would really like to have known who was in charge here. I found out later that it was an Indian Army general who had returned from the battles along the Tigris. There is no doubt in my mind that his bad organisation led to poor and delayed supply and had a devastating effect on our troops and the whole war operation. Why didn't he take urgent action?

Basra was also a town of many thousands of people of several nationalities but why they chose to live in this unhealthy place was way beyond me. The weather was appalling; rain and cold through the winter and subsequent flooding of the river provided a breeding ground for mosquitoes. Consequently, the war followed the river as most of the surrounding land was almost impassable. In the summer, this land was one of the hottest parts of the world. This place, if properly cared for with efficient irrigation and organisation, could have been one of the loveliest places in the world, and in fact, at one time, it probably was. Exotic palm trees laid claim to its better times. It was no coincidence that the legendary Garden of Eden was to be found a little further up the Tigris at Qurna.

The Indian Army had launched the campaign in Mesopotamia and I must admit, they were doing a very good job so far. We had made impressive advances towards Baghdad but had been stopped at Ctesiphon just a handful of miles away and we were now retreating down the River Tigris. But there was no back up: few basic supplies such as food and weapons and no medical equipment: no logistical plan at all. There was no doubt that we had over-stretched ourselves by advancing too far too fast. Our supplies were, of course, far too late and no help at all to the poor men of Kut who were now prisoners of the dreaded Turks, but would be invaluable to our new forces now trying to reverse our fortunes here.

There were rudimentary hospitals here and further up at Amara, but they were not suitable for our casualties and had almost no medical equipment nor medicines and very few nurses or doctors. The incidence of disease was more serious than the casualties of fighting. I shuddered to think of all the men we had lost because we didn't look after them with proper care. There were thousands of cases of dysentery and sunstroke in addition to a host of other deadly diseases. We also needed more and better ships for transport up the Tigris, but I had heard that these had been asked for but were always held up.

The wounded should have been carried down the river in the larger hospital ships but there were far too few of them. They were overcrowded and almost as bad as the barges. There were thousands more casualties being brought down, more each day from the fierce battles to relieve Kut. They were dumped in these horrible barges. I wondered what would have happened if news of this reality had reached Fleet Street. There would be the biggest outcry from the people of Britain and changes would have been made and those responsible dismissed.

I was pleased when we finally got underway to India. We transported the wounded to Bombay which took just over a week travelling at a steady ten knots. I visited all the wounded during the trip and wanted to speak to Eddie to find out what had happened to him but the combination of his injuries and pain and probably the effect of the drugs we had given him, ensured that he slept most of the journey back and he was in no condition to talk. I owed him a huge debt of gratitude for his support several years ago which probably saved my life.

There were hordes of men waiting for us at the docks in Bombay on an extremely hot and muggy day. I had arranged for them to be ready for us and they rushed on board to collect the wounded. We had lost only three men on our journey which I think was a near miracle considering their condition and near starvation and they were the first to be taken off the ship when we docked there. All the men had been dehydrated and had survived days without food and we needed to repair their bodies. Their minds would take much longer to recover. It was a miracle we didn't lose more.

Using our stretchers, they carried the men off the ship for the short journey to the train station. They worked quickly and carefully. There were some more seriously sick and wounded who we thought were not up to the long journey to the north and I arranged for them to be taken to the General Hospital at Bombay. I had requisitioned a train for the wounded and had adapted it with beds and privacy curtains so that the journey would be as comfortable as possible. I also built an operating theatre into one of the carriages which was used almost constantly during the several days it took us to travel to Simla some one thousand miles away. Meanwhile, the dockside team were responsible for cleaning and disinfecting the steamer inside and out and carrying out small refurbishments. They were then to refuel with coal and reload the ship with essential supplies for our men in Mesopotamia. I should have left Eddie in Bombay, but I wanted to look after him myself. Some of the medical staff disagreed with me but I overruled them. I knew that he was a very tough character and a survivor.

I travelled on the train with the wounded to Simla to ensure a safe and comfortable trip. We didn't lose any men on the way and indeed I believe that the fresh mountain air and incredible views helped to keep their spirits up. We had a kitchen on the train and the men were well-fed and watered by an excellent chef. They were relieved to be away from the horrors of Kut and for many of them, a year of almost constant fighting. Unfortunately, we had to change trains a couple of times and needed to transfer the equipment and connect the operating theatre with the new train. The long barge journey was now a distant nightmare. Nevertheless, the train journey was exhausting, and we were all grateful when it was finally over. We transported the wounded to a large hospital which was some distance away at the edge of this beautiful city. This time, we used horses and carts making the men as comfortable as possible.

When the wounded were settled and had slept off the effects of the journey, I visited them all before I had to make the long journey back to Bombay where the team would have completed the loading and repairs to the ship and had carried enough coal on board for the return journey.

Before I left, I had a very short conversation with Eddie who was now a little better and was sitting up in bed although it would take many months of care for him to recover his health fully after his dreadful ordeal. He was, of course, still terribly disfigured, but the surgeons had performed a miracle in repairing his face. I had huge respect for these craftsmen and had watched them at work. They used a new technique called skin grafting—new to me but Hindu doctors had been carrying out similar practices for over a thousand years. The surgeons had taken skin from other parts of his body, mainly his backside and had layered it onto his face. The skin started to grow and settle almost immediately. It was hard to keep up with all the modern-day technology: our Victorian fathers would not have believed this was possible.

"Those bastards have taken skin from my Khyber Pass and plastered it onto my Boat Race!" he was fond of saying later.

Eddie was slight but tall and he was vast in character and sense of humour. He made the whole ward laugh with his jokes and stories. Most of his tales were extremely improbable and could not be repeated in decent company. Indeed, we used to say we had to clear out the nurses and clergymen before he got started. He often said that he had kept the men in stitches, but he was very good in keeping morale high in the group and I am sure he aided recovery. However, I was aware that he was still very weak and slept much of the time.

"I ask the nurses for a kiss on my cheek and then I tell them they've just kissed me arse! You should see them recoil after that!"

When I could get him to talk seriously, I enjoyed catching up on the intervening years. He was now a lieutenant colonel in the Ox and Bucks Regiment serving in the Sixth Poona Division but had only arrived there just after the start of the war. He served overseas before that and he was a bit evasive about the activities he was involved in. It sounded like undercover work and I determined to question him more about this. Back home, he kept a flat near the Oval in South London (it's extraordinary that our homes were only a couple of miles apart) and his many escapades were revealed in his stories. He had been a womaniser and gambler and experienced many hair-raising adventures. One story involved him climbing out of the window of his flat and scaling the wall to avoid some rather unpleasant gambling debt collectors. On another occasion, he carried out a similar exercise to avoid an irate husband. This time, he was clinging to the side of the building as bare as a new-born babe. Well, he put it a bit more crudely!

Amazingly he was now married, and the wedding had taken place in Holland in 1912. I'm not sure where he met Lavinia Wilhelmina Van Toll, better known as Molly, but he said she was related to Dutch royalty. Molly now lived with her family in Holland and intended to stay there for the duration of the war. He was extremely worried about her as, unsurprisingly, he had not heard from her for several months. I arranged for him and all the other men to write letters to their loved ones and we had a good postal system to Britain, much better than the service offered in Mesopotamia, or Mespot as all the men called the country. The men were all very anxious to reassure their families that they were all right and missing them and of course when they received letters from home, their condition magically improved. Eddie needed many months of personal care which we couldn't offer so I asked him if there was anyone he knew who could look after him here. He told me that his sister, Amicia, was a trained nurse and might come out to care for him. The journey would be difficult for a woman travelling on her own, but I encouraged him to write to her which he did.

Another time I asked him about his recent ordeal: "I wanted to thank you for saving my life. I don't remember much about the journey on that stinking barge, but I do remember crying out for water and pain relief, but those boys just ignored us. They never tried to keep the boat clean—just left us to stew. At times, it was terribly hot, but mostly, I slept or fell unconscious. I heard that the journey to Basra took five days and fortunately, the enemy did not try to stop us and there were no attacks. We had suffered a horrible journey over rough ground to get to the barge. We were in very basic carts pulled by mules and there was no suspension at all. I felt particularly sorry for men with broken limbs; one man had a smashed hip. They suffered worse pain than those tortured in the Tower of London in times gone by. The drivers never slowed up to allow for our injuries. I will never forget that terrible journey."

I would have really liked to have spoken to him some more, but it was time to return to Bombay for the next venture.

During the long interminable journey, I began to reflect on my life so far. It had certainly not been boring! My training and responsibility was concerned with logistics, the supply of goods and weapons to the front line. This had been my work for around twenty years since I had cut my teeth in South Africa as a junior lieutenant, just after first arriving in India. I had previously passed out from Woolwich Officer School in England.

Our main purpose in India was to keep the Russians out if they ever started threatening us. We knew they wanted the wealth of India for themselves. As a relatively small force, we could only hold out for a short time but enough, it was hoped, to delay them until reinforcements had arrived from other parts of India and from Britain. We were also responsible for internal peace and security.

Our third objective was to keep the Afghan tribesman under control and often had to chase them away from our territories. There seemed to be uprisings every few weeks and this involved our forces being sent to wild and desolate mountain areas and I had to ensure they had all the food and equipment they needed. I travelled on many expeditions into these areas and could write another book about my experiences in this North-West Frontier. Our lines often came under attack and we had to shoot our way out of tricky situations.

On one occasion, I was with a small group of six when we were cut off from the main force by tribesmen. They were picking us off with ease and within a brief time, we had lost three of our men. Thank goodness Havildar Singh was unhurt and he was extremely cool under intense fire. Singh was one of the bravest men I knew and he came from a long line of serving men. Both his father and grandfather had served with the British with great distinction in many campaigns. It was obvious to me that we would be overwhelmed in seconds when Singh stood up and roared with primordial power from the depths of his being and the deep, rasping boom sounded exactly like a wounded lion seeking revenge. I was shocked to my core and my skin shivered in sheer terror. As for our attackers who had been rushing towards us, they froze for a second, their faces became as white as chalk and their eyes bulged in horror. Singh used this instant advantage to charge the rabble whilst still roaring like a demented demon. They made an immediate unanimous decision not to confront this madman, dropped their weapons and turned tail running and crying as if an ancient spirit were let loose.

We could never completely defeat these tribesman as they seemed to vanish up into the hills and hidden caves. We had a very dangerous situation when our discarded Martini rifles had finished up in the hands of a rogue band of tribesmen from the North-West Frontier. We preferred to use the new Lee-Metford rifles and it seems that the former had been sold on the black market. It was a scandal that this had been allowed to happen, but we had to deal with the situation. Though discarded, the Martini or Martini-Henry to give it its correct title was a fine weapon with a range of a thousand yards. We used to hold all the heights within three hundred yards of a column, but this was now not enough, and the situation caused us huge logistical problems. They used to pick off our men from greater distances and any wounded left behind could be tortured and castrated.

We spent many months hunting down and capturing or killing these tribesmen. We supported the artillery and our poor horses and mules had to haul these heavy guns hundreds of miles. We often had to climb steep mountains to gain a high place to bombard the enemy. For the higher peaks, we often used a new kind of gun which could be taken apart and my men would make the exhausting climb, carrying the gun parts up thousands of feet and then reassembling the weapons. These were breech loading quick fire ten pounders, much smaller than our regular artillery but ideal for mountain warfare. We used oxen to haul the heavier guns along the great flat plains and I used to watch the Hindu drivers to ensure they did not harm the animals. They were known for twisting the oxen tails to make them perform better. I only saw this happen once and after I acted, the driver never worked for us again.

We used the heliograph to communicate between our forces and coordinating our artillery in the hills and mountains. This simple flashing light system served us very well and we continued to use the technology for many years even though this was largely superseded by the telegraph system. Technology had advanced with the most extraordinary speed. Can you imagine that only a few years ago sending a letter to London and a getting a reply could take up to two years involving a long hazardous journey around the Cape and back again, also being delayed by a slow decision-making process? It was no wonder that India became almost autonomous from England during this time. Then later, after 1860, when the Suez Canal was built, a letter could be taken straight through to Marseille and then by train to Calais and London the time required had been reduced to around six weeks. Now with the Indo-Iranian telegraph line, communications could be reduced to a few hours. Surely, there could never again be such dramatic advances in technology in such a short space of time. We were then much more closely monitored and less independent. We were also communicating by telegraph between our centres in India and across continents and countries, and this was extremely useful for our forthcoming venture into Mesopotamia.

Away from the troubles, I lived mostly in the officer compound in Murree which had been the headquarters in times past before moving to Simla. We were closer to the problem areas here. Life was generally good and very sociable: we hunted, played polo and wacked rubber balls against mud walls in underground bunkers. Our Indian men became devilish good at this game and it became almost impossible to beat them. We worked, played and partied alongside our troops and grew to love them like brothers. We were still wary of some castes and religions and even though the terrible mutiny took place long ago in 1857, the stories were vividly passed down by senior members of the regiment and the horrors were recalled. We thought that talk of this terrible time would be discouraged but the events were recalled with pride. Everything changed after the mutiny and new rules were brought in: no proselytising (trying to change someone's religion) and indeed we were ordered to insist that our men's religions were strictly observed: the proportion of British to Indian troops should never fall below one to three. There were many other new rules which were strictly enforced.

I enjoyed my life and work in India although at times it was incredibly hard and demanding and the elements were harsh. My work consumed my time and energy and challenged me to my core. The weather and terrain could be fierce, and I am sure that mine and my colleagues' health suffered and many of our lives were shortened as a result. I loved the sights and smells of the country and the beautiful trees and flowers. Above all, I loved the food: our Indian servants cooked and served us the most delicious dishes; their skills in the use of spices, herbs and blends were totally different from the rather bland food I had been used to in England. I would have hated to go back to those plain dishes. I think my biggest love was reserved for the animals, the horses and domestic dogs we cared for. There were, of course, a huge variety of wild animals including elephants and tigers, but my favourites were the cheeky monkeys and the way they copied all our limb movements would reduce us to tears of laughter. I loved the colourful birds too and I think in another life I would have trained as an animal carer or vet. I hoped one day I could afford a small farm in England where I could keep horses. I would build a duck pond and sit and watch these comical colourful birds as they waddled and paddled searching for the next feed. I should not daydream like this too much! My other love was flowers and gardens and I had a couple of acres at the back of my bungalow. I worked in my garden whenever I had the time and I was helped by my full-time gardener or perhaps I should say I assisted him on rare occasions.

I have often been asked about the politics of the Raj and our occupation of a foreign country and its people. We had been here for hundreds of years and so it was difficult to judge the rights and wrongs of this, but I was hugely proud of all the good we had brought to India. The people had always suffered from terrible diseases such as cholera, typhoid and malaria and all kinds of stomach issues which were made worse by the famines, crop failures and droughts. By the time I arrived in India, we had already built around twenty-five thousand miles of railway which carried essential food to millions and our new canal and irrigation systems had made available over ten million acres of new cultivated land. We had carried out extensive civil engineering projects including roads and bridges. We had brought over thousands of trained administrators and civil servants and had improved the health and education of the nation. We increased the wealth of the nation for the benefit not only of Britain but certainly for the people of India. We also protected the nation from warlike warriors and robbers on its borders. Nevertheless, we were aware of negative opinions from some left-wing politicians at home and there were always rumblings of discontent from some of the natives.

The memories of the great rebellion of 1857 had never really gone away, and we faced minor rebellions during my early years there. It was plain to me that one day, perhaps quite soon, we must hand over this beautiful country to its rightful owners and occupants. I sincerely hoped I would not be here when that day came as I could see terrible trouble ahead. There were so many religions and castes which would oppose and fight each other without our security that many believed the country could be destroyed in a terrible civil war. There would have to be new territories created to separate these people for their own safety. Yet, despite all this, we had a good relationship with the vast majority of the people and I know I can count on many hundreds as good friends. I treated all the people with great respect as equals regardless of their situation although I must agree that not all my fellow British did the same. Some of them were cruel to the native people and treated them as inferior beings, often less than beasts. I always stood up for the people against these uneducated types although I was only effective when they were junior to me. I told my troops that we were all members of the highest caste—the caste of soldiers. I rarely had trouble with the troops I led.

I attended several of the magnificent durbars in Delhi where we displayed the power and pageantry of the British nation. I was called in to help with the supply and design of these ceremonies. The greatest of these was the celebrations during the visit of our King George V as Emperor of India and his wife, Mary. No expense was spared on this important occasion and we were determined to impress the nation. Indian princes queued up to pay homage to this great king who was the grandson of the fabled Empress of India Victoria. This was the first time our reigning monarch had visited the country and we commemorated with a show of such extravagance which exceeded anything which had taken place before. The king and queen sat on golden thrones in purple robes and thousands of our red-coated soldiers paraded proudly in front of crowds of more than one hundred thousand. Afterwards, the king went hunting on a magnificent elephant and his entourage killed many tigers and bears, much to my disapproval and disappointment. Nevertheless, the show of British supremacy and influence was very powerful and spectacular. I remember having thousands of these uniforms made at huge expense and ordering the creation of a massive marquee in Madras.

I also served further south in Poona for a couple of years where the weather was uncomfortably hot and humid. I was always happy to travel back up north. During the first part of the Great War, I travelled extensively around the country searching for and buying goods for the use of our army in Mesopotamia. Some of the products were quite specialised; for example, I used to travel to Calcutta to buy jute sacks. They could be used to carry all kinds of food and other items and jute was the perfect material for this. Jute is a natural product and is grown in the Bengal province and made up in local mills. I researched the mills for the most appropriate manufacturer and settled on one owned by a Mr Dutta. He gave me the best deal overall and could supply the vast volume I required. He also offered to ship his bags to Bombay so that we could then carry them to Mesopotamia. I did business with him for many years and I was pleased to learn years later that he had become one of the wealthiest and generous benefactors in India. There were dozens of other products we had to supply from across the country for our war effort and of course we had to obtain the very best prices and avoid being cheated. We could not source too much from our mother country as the supply took too long and was expensive.

I also had to find animals for our army: we used to bring them in from England, but the poor animals were often in a terrible state by the time they got to us and many were sadly lost. The Indian horses were of poor quality: small and skinny and no use to our army. We had also brought in good horses from Asia but had to take them through Afghan passes which had its obvious problems which were even more difficult when relationships were bad. I was delighted to oversee a Remount unit near to Murree. This was rather like a British stud where we bred strong sturdy horses for our cavalry and tough horses for our artillery teams. We also bred mules and donkeys for their tough duties. I always insisted on good treatment for all our animals and I once hit a man with my stick for abusing a beautiful foal. I then sacked him from his job and ensured that he never came near to the stud again. The men soon understood that they had to maintain the highest standards of care and welfare for these lovely animals. After a while, this was our sole source of supply in India and for our army in Mesopotamia. These were my favourite responsibilities during my time in India and I knew that my ideal future would be the welfare of animals.

I was so relieved not to be working in the bank with my father. He drilled into me that I must follow him in his career, but I really didn't want to spend my life in a dusty office in Brixton where we lived, and he worked. He also nagged my younger brother, Stanley, who eventually had the sense to immigrate to Canada. I never saw him again. One day, I had a big showdown with my father: he insisted once again that I obey him whilst holding a big threatening stick. I blurted out that I was going to become an officer in the British Army. He laughed and dropped his stick:

"You won't last five minutes in the army. How are you going to pay for your uniform and equipment and how about your mess bills? Don't think that I will be funding you because I won't!"

"It's not like that now," I spluttered unconvincingly.

I can still hear his wheedling voice, sounding rather like a school headmaster. He was right of course: you needed a private income to be an officer and the pay was lousy. There was no way he was going to fund me although he could certainly have afforded to. When that dreadful interview was over, I found out from a friend that the Indian Army paid far more than our own army and much of one's equipment was free. I had no inheritance or land, so this seemed to be my best choice and I was very excited at the possibility. In time, I could return to England with a pile of money, buy some land and build a house. I could live on a small pension. I made some enquiries, joined the Officer School and travelled to India to seek my fortune. Unfortunately, the deal was nowhere near as good as I was led to believe but I had to find out the hard way. The pay turned out to be reasonable and the life in India was very low cost but there was certainly no fortune to be made and my future pension looked grim, but that was, of course, far too far ahead to worry about. I was able to afford two servants, so life was quite good. I always worked hard for the next promotion which meant improvements in pay and conditions. Some of my fellow officers enjoyed a private income from their families and were able to live a very good life. A few were able to afford a team of polo ponies but for me, this was out of the question. I never saw my father or mother again.

The only drawback to my life in India was the scarcity of the opposite sex, well—suitable girls anyway. When I was in Simla and Murree, the social life was very lively as many officers and their wives came here for relief from the heat of the plains and steaming unhealthy jungles. I did not care for dances and heavy drinking, but this certainly was a good place to meet people and socialise. Many of my fellow officers were married and a few played the field so to speak, often with married ladies when their officer husbands were away and took terrible risks. I remember a husband coming home unexpectedly and found some bounder in bed with his wife. The man was drummed out of the army and was forced to go back home. We never heard from him again. Of course, I would never do anything like that but life there could be very lonely. The only other option was to go native, but this was not what I wanted.

I made another six journeys to Basra over many months and while they were without memorable incident, I was pleased to see huge improvements had been made on the docks which had been extended and rebuilt. We could now unload several ships at once. There were many more dockers there and plenty of working cranes. Also, very close to the docks a new hospital was being built and there was less need to transfer and treat all the wounded in India. Britain had now taken over the running of the campaign from the Indian administration and the whole organisation had improved dramatically.

On the third occasion, I was ordered to command a river steamer up the Tigris carrying essential supplies to our men at Kut which we had just recaptured. I detailed my second in command to take our ship back to Bombay. Our army had been very successful in recent months defeating the enemy in a number of battles. We were now better organised, better supplied and our wounded were cared for in a much more humane way. I didn't know it at the time, but I was to make many further trips up the Tigris to Kut and beyond to bring supplies from Basra and to take the wounded back. We took the majority of our wounded to the new hospital in Basra where they were looked after as well as we could in Simla. We now had many good British nurses and doctors there.

I was interested to see the places on the way and having heard so many stories from the men I had looked after, I felt I knew the river as well as they did. Eddie had told me about Qurna and I was deeply moved knowing that this was the probable site of the Garden of Eden although it was far from being the nirvana described in the Bible. We finally arrived in Kut. We navigated the huge loop around the town which incidentally was still a bombed-out wreck. It was easy to see that that this was not a place of safety for our army but a dangerous trap for the twenty-thousand people inside. I felt dreadful when I thought of our men starving and dying of disease in this miserable dirty place. However, I was relieved that Kut was now back in our hands. We had also taken Baghdad and were now moving north to defeat the Ottomans. I made the return journey down the Tigris to Basra.

I travelled back to Basra and caught a lift in another ship just about to make the journey to Bombay and then on to Simla. As I looked back at the port of Basra as we slowly moved along the Shatt Al Arab, I reflected on my extraordinary experiences here and the terrible sacrifices our men had made to secure this country they called Mespot. I thought about Eddie and the awful day his barge came into the docks. I had an uneventful trip back home. I was to return to Mesopotamia and by river to Baghdad twice more. My main mission now was to improve the supply of goods to our men there after the disgraceful history of our earlier venture. The need to carry the wounded and sick had lessened considerably.

Eddie's sister, Amicia, had at last arrived in Simla after an arduous journey from England. It was unheard of for a lady to travel on her own halfway across the world and during the most fierce and terrible war the world had ever seen. She was indeed a most extraordinary person and a lovely lady. I picked her up from the station in my horse drawn Dak Tonga carriage and lifted her one small suitcase into the space at the back. She was unsurprisingly extremely tired and I took her towards the accommodation I had arranged for her. She was to stay with a soldier friend's family. They had a large bungalow adjacent to the barracks. When we arrived there, she asked where the hospital was and when I told her it was five miles to the north, she insisted on being taken there immediately. I foolishly suggested she rested first and settle in.

"Nonsense. I want to see Eddie immediately. I have travelled thousands of miles and do not want to waste another minute."

I was to become used to her determined character and dare I say it—obstinacy over the next couple of years. Of course, I obeyed and went straight to the hospital. The journey in the warm evening sunshine was lovely and we chatted easily. Of course, she wanted to know everything about Eddie's health and I updated her as well as I could, not being medically trained. She asked me dozens of questions and I stumbled on some of the medical ones. There was time to hear about her journey in a troop ship which was quite extraordinary and very dangerous. I also wanted to know more about her but found out little as she kept asking me questions about life in India and the war in general. We got to the hospital far too quickly and I determined to talk to her some more, but I was due to leave in a couple of days.

I took her up to Eddie's ward but wouldn't go in with her. It was their private moment.

I sat outside the ward and patiently waited for Amicia to come out. This gave me valuable time to reflect on all that had happened in the past few months and the extraordinary story of Eddie's survival. My thoughts drifted back some twenty years to those terrible times in Africa and where I met Eddie for the first time in Ladysmith. He had provided me with an extremely valuable service at great personal risk and had probably saved my life. I was very pleased to have helped him in return in his hour of great distress and sickness. I hoped that now Amicia could nurse him back to full health over the next few months and years.

I remembered the sights and smells of that great country and in the warmth of the waiting room, I must have drifted into a deep sleep.

South Africa:
Herbert's First War

Lived a woman wonderful
(May the Lord amend her!)
Neither simple, kind, nor true,
But her Pagan beauty drew
Christian gentlemen a few
Hotly to attend her.

Christian gentlemen a few
From Berwick unto Dover;
For she was South Africa,
And she was South Africa,
She was Our South Africa,
Africa all over!

Rudyard Kipling

Herbert Messenger in South Africa

I heard one shot which cracked with deafening loudness and zinged towards us like an angry bee and in an instant, our major was dead. His eyes bulged in shock and his mouth formed an O of surprise as he was flung backwards off his horse crashing onto the dusty ground. His horse whinnied and moved away as if to avoid the next attack. The major did not move, and his blood was pumping into the ground from the dreadful rent in his chest. We were too shocked to react for a long second until a crackling of fierce shots and ricochets broke the silence and our stupor. I yelled to the men to get behind the wagons for cover. We kicked up huge piles of dust which helped to shield our escape as we dragged our mounts to safety. The drivers jumped down to conceal themselves. While we scrambled to safety, I heard the scream of a horse which bucked and threw its rider on to the ground. He picked himself up and then scurried to safety with the rest of us. The horse had been hit in the rump and was writhing and moaning in pain. I hated to see animals suffering and I had witnessed so many horrible animal deaths. Men dying were bad enough, but animals were the sentient innocents in these wars. I raised my rifle and shot the poor creature through its brain killing it instantly. Luckily, the other horses survived and were led to safety. I peered between the wagons and saw the small rocky mound ahead and to the right where I thought the shots had come from.

It was only then that I realised I was now the senior officer here and had to take command of these men: three were young British officers and the rest were Indians from the Punjab we had brought with us. Their leader was Havildar Singh who I had worked with since my arrival in India only two years ago. I knew I could rely on him totally and I was relieved to have him with me. This was the first time I had been fired on in anger as it was often described. I wasn't frightened yet as everything had happened too quickly to affect me. Maybe when I had time to reflect later…

"Keep your heads down!" Singh shouted. It suddenly dawned on me that he was my havildar now that the major was dead.

More shots rang out and I knew they were firing Mauser rifles with deadly accuracy. These were ruthless weapons and superior to our own and could be fired rapidly without making smoke deposits.

"How many are there?" I asked him.

"At least a dozen, sir." This was bad news. We outnumbered them with around twenty men plus our drivers, but we were up against Boers who lived, farmed and hunted in these lands. They had outsmarted our far bigger armies and had made our leaders look foolish. My Indians were not fighting men as an agreement had been reached at the outset of the campaign that neither side would arm native and non-white troops. Both sides feared the outcome if the brown or black people, who greatly outnumbered the whites on both sides, took up arms against them on either side.

I heard that this rule had been broken by both sides particularly in dangerous situations. It didn't take me long to realise that we were in one of those.

"Havildar, order one man to get into this wagon and take out rifles for each man."

As usual, he was ahead of me and had just ordered one man to do exactly this…I would learn that he always had a knack of anticipating my orders. In a minute, each man was armed and under his command, they were rapidly firing back into the mound but having negligible effect so far.

In all the excitement, I felt extremely hot and suddenly thirsty. It was a relentlessly blazing and cloudless day and the action had caused extreme tension and sweat on my head and over my whole body. I ordered water bottles to be passed to the men.

"Keep your heads down," Havildar Singh yelled again and just then one man's head flicked backwards and he fell with a bullet in his brain. We needed no more reminders after this. The Boer firing was continuous and relentless and very accurate.

"Can we outflank them?" I asked him.

"We have no cover out there. Let me think."

After a few moments he said, "We have some pom-poms in the end wagon. We could fire them into the enemy and blow them away."

I thought for a moment and remembered that these guns were normally used by the Boers, but we had captured half a dozen of them a few weeks back. They were converted Maxim machine guns which could fire one-pound shells. They were usually only used against armoured vehicles or fortifications but there was no reason why we couldn't use them to have a blast at these Boers.

"Good idea, Havildar. Take who you need and let's set one up to start with. Does anyone know how to use them?"

I got no answer but immediately, he led six men to the rear wagon and they climbed inside.

This gave me a few moments to reflect of the happenings of the past few months. I had been in India for two years with the S and T Corps, Supply and Transport, Indian Army based mostly in Simla and Murree after having completed my officer training at Woolwich. I remember how pleased and relieved I felt when I passed out from there. I could now look forward to escaping from a dreary life in the bank. I went to see my father to tell him that my departure to India was imminent and I wish I hadn't. He was sitting at his desk and he looked crestfallen.

It wasn't a happy meeting and I left under a bit of a cloud. My elder brother, Stanley, had seen sense and had immigrated to Canada. I would miss my dear mother terribly but little else. I joined the ship at Southampton and within a couple weeks, we had arrived at Bombay travelling via the Suez Canal. I travelled to Simla by train which took a couple of days. I was twenty-two years old and the year was 1897. This was an incredible experience for a young man.

I enjoyed my first two years in India until news of a fresh crisis loomed in South Africa. We were ordered to prepare for a long campaign and to buy and deliver goods to Calcutta. I had been trained in the logistics of such exercises but there was fear and immediacy in this reality. We travelled in the first convoy from Calcutta in the Purnea which was the leading ship. There were about twenty ships in this first venture and more had just left Bombay. It had taken about fifteen days to reach Durban where we were needed to defend our people there. We carried tons of equipment to support our army and this included guns, signalling, medical supplies and we even had a veterinary hospital on board. We carried live animals including thousands of horses and oxen and plenty of saddles and other equipment.

Each ship had a small army of men who spent their time cleaning and disinfecting the holds containing animals and collected tons of excrement to drop over the sides. Some of these poor animals became agitated and their fear spread to the others. There were many occasions when I was called to calm them before panic took over as I had a reputation for being able to communicate with them. The smell, of course, was terrible, and it was such a relief when I finally came up for sea air. We had a large part of the hold full of boots, in fact everything an army away from home needed. We could, of course, top up much of this locally but there was a continuous need for supply of equipment and horses from India throughout our campaign as well. I had enjoyed putting the logistics theory I had learnt into practice for the first time although it was a huge relief when we finally arrived in Durban.

We were led by Sir George White with around twelve thousand men, an equal number to the enemy, but already we had suffered setbacks in and around Ladysmith and we were forced back into the town. Many hundreds of our men were killed and wounded and they were besieged in Ladysmith. We were meant to protect Natal until the British forces arrived in Cape Town. So far, we had failed spectacularly.

The job of my team and I was to get these supplies to our troops as quickly and safely as possible. We were now unable to do so as the town was now encircled by thousands of the Boers.

The day was hotter than usual, but we weren't expecting any trouble as we believed that all the Boers were further forward blocking our way to Ladysmith. When we heard the first shot, we were taken by complete surprise.

The men quickly set up the pom-pom gun and loaded the first shot. They were exposed between two wagons to get sight of the enemy. The first shot fell some way short and the next too far to the right and then after adjustment too far to the left. My men gradually improved their skills. The fourth shell blasted right in front of the mound and a few heads popped up in alarm. We managed to shoot one of their men as we were waiting for the opportunity. I am sure the Boers were seriously concerned, and I ordered my havildar to mount up six of the men ready to charge them. Well, I didn't quite order him if the truth were known. It was more of a request or suggestion. I needed to know if it was a good idea. Just then, we made a direct hit with the pom-pom and some of their men started running away. That was our signal to charge and our men raced towards them shooting as they rode.

We killed two of them and the others, approximately seven men, scrambled for their horses, mounted them expertly and rode away fast. We called off the chase and I rode over to the mound. I was distraught to see that the dead men were only boys, perhaps only twelve or thirteen years old. These kinds of attacks were rare, and I assumed that this was a gang of children who were bored and thought they would have a few pot shots at the horrible British and maybe capture a small supply train. They were probably farm boys who had been riding and shooting since they were three. I stood for a moment deep in thought and sadness. I turned back and ordered the men to rest and eat, which they did in the shade of the wagons before we buried the dead in shallow graves. We then set off on our journey again. I was in a rather sombre mood.

The invasion force from England had arrived in Cape Town and made rapid progress towards Ladysmith. I heard we had twenty thousand men under General Sir Redvers Buller, several times more than the Boers and we were told that the war would be over by Christmas, just a couple of months away. This turned out to be extremely optimistic.

We had already witnessed the deadly skills of the Boer and these were only children. They were deadly shots and could move quickly on fast horses but were untrained soldiers. These men were farmers not fighters. They worked independently unlike the operation of the structured discipline of the soldiers of the British Army who reacted obediently to commands of their officers at all levels, however inappropriate they may have been. They had good Mauser guns which could fire quickly. It was said that the Boer had a Mauser in one hand and a Bible in the other.

We had poor out of date maps, were badly advised and had inexperienced leaders. We didn't know the land and of course they did. It was their land after all not ours. Our strategy was completely wrong, and our stubborn leaders would never admit this and kept compounding the errors.

I was not surprised when news had come in about the disasters we were suffering at the start of this war. It was not going to be over by Christmas.

We were besieged in three towns, in Kimberley, Mafeking and of course in Ladysmith where we were headed. Our invading army had split into three divisions to relieve each one of these.

Each division had suffered terrible losses of many thousands and many defeats. It seemed that our generals had not got a clue how to fight the Boer. One of our generals forgot he had left seven hundred men on a hill, got lost and then blamed his junior officers!

After a few uneventful days of travelling, we could hear the distant boom of our guns in the distance and we were heading towards our army. I prayed that we would start winning and this horrible war would soon be over.

I could see from my rudimentary map that we were approaching the Tugela River which twisted and turned sharply. I saw a dead soldier lying ahead on our path and then another dozen or so. I had a horrible premonition that I was about to witness the aftermath of a dreadful disaster. Our men were walking among them looking for those still alive and calling out when they saw movement. Doctors and stretchers bearers were attending to them and soon it was apparent to me that there were hundreds of victims.

Shortly afterwards, I heard the story from a colonel: the Boers were dug in on the banks of the River and we bombarded them for two days without much effect. I learned that our cavalry had galloped into an ambush and many were killed. It was decided to bring up our artillery to bombard the enemy close up. Teams of horses had drawn twelve guns close to the River. They ran out of shells and the ammunition carts were nowhere to be seen. Under heavy fire, the guns had to be abandoned.

A group of very brave men had ridden towards the guns and attempted to pull them away. They were under sustained attack from rifle and artillery fire and amazingly managed to pull two guns back to their lines. During this intense fighting, Frederick Roberts, Lord Robert's son, was killed. It was another humiliating defeat for our army with huge losses. This was known as the battle of Colenso: the series of defeats was known as Black Week.

I was told to report to another colonel about a mile towards the front and we unloaded supplies into a large tent. I was then ordered to return to Durban to bring back more supplies. I had an uneventful return journey and was back with the army in about four weeks. I could not believe the vast number of men now involved. Many thousands more had arrived from England landing at Cape Town and travelling to help with the relief of Ladysmith. As I arrived, the army was attempting to capture the highest peak in the mountain range known as Spion Kop. I had to take my wagons across the Tugela River which was in quite full flow. One wheel broke and the wagon keeled over. With great difficulty, we managed to lift the side of the wagon and secure a new wheel in place and we crossed without further incident.

I looked towards the range of huge craggy mountains and saw the rough steep slopes of Spion Kop. I could hear the thunderous booming of Boer artillery from adjacent peaks and the cracking of rifles. The air was full of acrid smoke and the atmosphere was terrifying. It was like the biggest firework party in the world multiplied by a factor of one hundred. We had been exposed to battle conditions during our training but had not experienced anything like this. Our men above us were experiencing very heavy fire and the whole mountain was shaking. I was told that our men had been fighting there since the early hours and were totally exposed to deadly Boer fire.

We moved toward the daunting slopes of Spion Kop and I wondered how our men had managed to climb its steep and stony sides. Due to the vastness of the mountain, we could not see the peak. I watched as a young chap dressed in khaki skidded and scrambled down the mountain and made his way quickly to the general's camp. Some minutes later, he came back to the foot of the mountain where my men and I were standing.

The man shouted, "We desperately need water for the men. Without water they will be forced to surrender."

I offered my services immediately.

"I have mules and plenty of water bags. We can take them up now."

"The slopes are too steep for mules. We tried to carry arms up earlier and the mules fell backwards," he stated.

"We still must try. We can't carry enough water up without them. I will look for a more gradual slope."

I ordered twenty mules to be loaded up with the huge goatskins of water. Meanwhile, the man said that stretcher bearers were needed to bring the wounded back down. They were exposed to severe enemy fire and intense heat and urgently needed rescuing.

As we moved around the base of the mountain looking for gentler slopes, the man followed me and brought with him a group of around one hundred Indians with stretchers.

As we climbed, the man told me that he was Winston Churchill. I should have recognised him as he was well-known for his daring exploits in Africa as well as in many trouble spots around the World. Winston had fought in Cuba and in the Sudan and at the battle of Omdurman. Before that he had fought in the North-West Frontier of India which was my territory. He had been involved in fierce fighting there. More recently, he had been on board an armoured train which was captured by the Boers. He escaped from prison in Pretoria and had walked three hundred miles to freedom and since then had been made a lieutenant in the South African Light Horse. Winston had been a war reporter and I knew of him through his lively newspaper articles and I had seen his photograph several times. He had become a minor national hero. We had plenty of time to talk during the tough climb.

Walking alongside him was the leader of the Indian stretcher bearers. He was a young slight man who managed the steep slopes with ease (I didn't. I struggled upwards and spoke while breathing heavily!). He was called Mohandas Gandhi and had lived in South Africa for many years. He had got permission to start the Indian Ambulance Corps. He was fiercely loyal to Britain and spoke fondly of his relationships with the British people. I was extremely impressed with his devotion to duty and to the leadership he demonstrated to his men. The three of us had a most stimulating conversation during our exhausting climb upwards.

Winston told us about the situation on the top of Spion Kop: "They thought Spion Kop was the highest point, but they climbed up in the early morning in the dark and mist only to find that they were being fired on from three higher surrounding peaks. The men had tried to dig trenches but had hit rock after a few inches and the shallow trenches had provided limited protection—in fact almost none. Hardly enough depth to bury them when they fell but they were laid into these small trenches and covered with earth. The men had also been charged at from another part of Spion Kop by Boers using their rifle butts and huge knives. Then our men were constantly shelled and fired upon by the deadly Boer Mausers. They had no help from their generals and to compound their errors they had created confusion about who was in charge up there. Yet, still they are bravely resisting! I will prepare an article for the Morning Post and it won't be kind to our superiors."

I asked Winston what his plans were when the war was over.

"Well, I need to find an occupation to earn enough to keep me well-fed and watered as I am accustomed to. I've often dreamed about owning a share or two in a gold or diamond mine, just big enough to keep me in whisky and champagne. I also fancy going into politics as my father did but only after I have had more world experience. Too many of our politicians only see the world through misty windows while slouching in their armchairs. I am sure I can do better than this current lot, but I still have much to learn. I don't think they really understand our great empire and how we can and should support and expand it. As a journalist, I have developed a love of writing and reckon I have a book or two in me."

Later he went on:

"We have made a dreadful mess of this war and I want to expose our leaders' incompetence to our people. They will be horrified when they know the extent of our failures. We need to rethink how we train our men for battle and how we structure our army. I suppose its many years since we have been involved in such a huge and long campaign. I guess the last time was in the Crimea and that was before our time."

"I don't support our hatred for the Boer," he went on. "It shows a dark side of our character. We should treat them with more generosity and tolerance and bring about a speedy peace as soon as we can."

Our mules could go no further. My men had to take off the goatskins and drag them, two men to a bag, up towards our stranded men at the top. I took a corner of a bag and dragged it upwards with Winston taking the other corner. My body was drenched in sweat and I was breathing hard. I don't think I have ever felt more tired and exhausted in my life. We still had a long way to go and I despaired to see the even steeper path and the impossible distance to the top.

When we finally reached the top, I was not prepared for the extent of the devastation laid out before us. We saw dozens of our dead, most mutilated by Boer guns. Many more were wounded, and Gandhi quickly led his men to them ignoring the dangerously close Mauser fire and the whining shells. I was amazed with the sight of the huge battlefield before me: I had not imagined anything like this. Winston immediately sought out Lt Col Thorneycroft who was fighting a desperate battle to save his men. The noise was deafening and the whole mountain shook with the artillery barrage and I choked on the thick acrid smoke swirling around the summit. I saw that most of the men were lying in shallow trenches and were exposed to fire from three close peaks and lines of Boers higher up on Spion Kop were firing at our exposed men. It was easy to see that they could not last long without reinforcements and that this was another British cock up like so many before. Thorneycroft had very poor support from the generals and intermittent or often no communication and indeed conflicting messages. It was Winston's initiative to climb up to find out his needs in addition to bringing him much needed water, stretcher bearers and information that one thousand four hundred reinforcements were on their way.

We quickly brought the goatskins to the men who were in desperate need of water. They waited their turn with admirable patience and ignored the bullets zinging around us. We had to ignore them as well but during our short stay up there, two of our men were cut down and badly wounded. Suddenly, the shooting stopped as the Boers could see that we were removing our wounded and I could see them climbing out of their trenches to rescue their own. Both sides were showing truce flags. Many of their wounded were stranded between the fighting armies because of their last failed charge. Gandhi and his men were working quickly and efficiently. I briefly wondered how they were going to take the wounded down the steep slopes.

Our job was soon done, and Winston walked up to us and told us to start our return journey. I was reluctant to leave the hundreds of brave men who were holding out here but knew I would be little use to them. I determined to return and bring more water and medical supplies and some badly needed food. Our return journey downhill was much easier without the heavy water bags.

"How did you get on with Thorneycroft?" I asked as we started our descent.

"He is doing a very courageous service for our country in impossible circumstances: his support from below is appallingly bad: General Warren hasn't replied to his urgent messages. He shouldn't be up here in the first instance as he's been sent to the wrong mountain. We should have known that. We should have sent up a reconnaissance balloon beforehand and then they would have seen the error of choosing this part of Spion Kop. He is very close to withdrawing and I suppose he will be in deep trouble for doing so. He has been asking for reinforcements for hours and they'd better be here very soon."

Winston was bright red in the face as he poured out his frustrations to me. He was determined to send his report to the Morning Post and he promised to spare no one he thought responsible even if he brought trouble for himself.

When he calmed down somewhat, he asked me what I knew about Gandhi. I said that I had only met him today and hadn't heard about him or his Ambulance Corps before. Winston told me that Gandhi had great ambitions to return to India and lead his country to independence. I didn't know whether to believe him but had no reason not to.

"He could be a very dangerous man and we need to keep an eye on him. He has great charisma and huge support from his people. Having said that he is doing an incredible job here and has saved many British lives so all credit to him for that. But he is certainly one to watch." He went on to tell me about Gandhi's early life and the development of his determination and extraordinary vision. I looked again at Gandhi and he seemed so young and unworldly that I found it hard to relate this young slight man to a potentially dangerous revolutionary.

The descent seemed to go very quickly as I was absorbed with our conversation. I saw that Gandhi and his men were taking very great care of the wounded and had not dropped any of the men. With the difficulty of negotiating the steep slope, this was an extraordinary achievement.

Just before we reached level ground, Winston asked me what my plans were. I told him why I had joined the Indian Army and that I had intended to make a long career of this. It wasn't an easy option, but I was committed to making a success of my commission and gain promotion.

"Yes, but what about the longer term."

"I want to return to my country one day but not until I have sufficient funds to do so. I eventually want to buy land and raise a family. In the meantime, I will serve my country to the best of my ability," I replied. I was conscious that my ambitions were not as great and worthy as his or even Gandhi's. I need not have worried.

"I wish I was half as loyal and selfless as you. I am more concerned about my consumption of alcohol and food, to ensure I have plenty. With people like you I am very optimistic for the future of our country."

I was aware of his extraordinary career to date: he had faced fierce enemies many times in several parts of the world and had displayed enormous courage and coolness as he had demonstrated already today. There was no doubt I had been privileged to meet a rising star, in fact two stars who would become hugely significant world players.

We repeated our climb once again with more water and supplies for the poor men above us and Gandhi and his men came with us. Winston was off—no doubt to write and send his column to the Morning Post. I know he was itching to do this as soon as possible.

As I was riding away from the scene hours later, I had plenty to reflect upon: we saw a battalion waiting at the base of Spion Kop for its final orders to climb the mountain to relieve Thorneycroft's beleaguered men. A colonel approached me and said I must report to a certain brigadier in his tent immediately. He pointed to a tent and I went there straight away. The brigadier gave me a fierce telling off for being absent without permission. It did not seem to matter what the urgent situation was or that I had brought much needed water to desperate men. That, I thought, was part of the problem with the army and if we all waited for orders and obeyed them to the letter—or perhaps that's what most of us did. There was little place for initiative. I thought for a moment he was going to reduce me to the ranks— he threatened to do so—but told me that my file was marked and that this insubordination would be entered on my record. He was reddening in the face as he shouted at me and some of his spittle sprayed in my direction. Just then Winston ducked into the tent and shouted:

"That was a superb show, Messenger, well done! I'm going to mention your actions and bravery in my next dispatch. You have saved many lives today."

He then ducked out again and that was the last I saw of him. The brigadier spluttered and told me I was dismissed from his presence! I didn't think his threats would go any further.

Later, I was ordered to make another trip to Durban for more supplies. I was able to reflect on the dreadful circumstances of our men on Spion Kop and the terrible loss of life there and on other recent disasters since we came to this country. We heard later that as the relieving battalion approached the top of the mountain, Thorneycroft had decided to give up. His men were exhausted, and he told the new arrivals that he had done all he could. The British all came back down.

As it happened, the Boers had also decided to give up and left believing that they had been defeated. Both sides, therefore, had deserted the top. When a Boer scouting group realised that the British had gone they rushed down to tell their comrades and they immediately reoccupied the summit. The irony is that the battle had already been won by us. What a disaster!

On my long trek, I also had time to take a very good look at the countryside and I was daydreaming about the future: this really was a very beautiful land with an abundance of nature. I saw dramatic wide horizons, thick forests and sparkling rivers, all surrounded by ranges of huge mountains. At that moment, a herd of antelope was moving slowly alongside our wagons heading to the north. They ignored us completely. I could see over what seemed to be one hundred miles in each direction and two mountain ranges. This was a vast fertile country and I daydreamed about moving here and settling down with a few acres of land. I could perhaps build a small ranch and raise a family. Where would I meet my wife? Then I thought of all the hatred and prejudice in the land, not just between the people of colour but between whites as well. Indeed, this was the reason this war was being fought: to bring equality to all people.

Newly arrived British people had fewer rights than the Dutch settlers and a huge political row ensued with no side giving way. Well, it just wasn't going to happen as we had hoped and worst of all, the black people were going to get a very bad deal indeed. Many of them had helped us and many had died in our cause, but they would remain very much second-class citizens in their own country. They were often treated even worse by the Boers. It didn't take me long to dismiss my dreams.

I thought about the progress of the war and the likely result. Sheer weight of British numbers had to win the day eventually although with the skills and adaptability of the Boers this was never going to be an easy task. What would happen then? I was looking forward to the ending so that I could return to my job in India. I wanted to go back very badly indeed.

My havildar called to me, "Sir, riders are coming. I think they are friendly."

I turned around and saw two riders galloping towards us from the way we had come. I could see they were not Boers but what on earth could they want with us? I would find out soon enough.

"Sir, our main wagon train has been captured by the Boers. We have lost the majority of the supplies we had," Second Lieutenant Browning told me. I vaguely wondered why he had addressed me as his senior as we were of equal rank.

I knew that our new leaders Kitchener and Roberts had changed the supply strategy: instead of each battalion making their own localised supply arrangements, there would be one supply chain for each army. Browning explained that this army was on its way to Bloemfontein with an enormous wagon train. The Boers had charged the oxen which were grazing nearby and more than three thousand were stampeded. It was a terrible loss for us but fortunately the valuable supplies were saved.

Browning's main orders from his superiors was for me to acquire thirty more wagons in addition to my existing twelve together with more supplies which were urgently needed. A company of soldiers would be arranged to guard my column and he had already telegraphed ahead to arrange this in Durban. I would be in total charge of this new column together with my new guards.

"Oh, and I was asked to tell you that you have been promoted to full lieutenant with immediate effect. You can pick up this order when you return to us. Hopefully, we will be in Ladysmith by then. Many congratulations, sir!" Browning delivered this good news.

Once again, my trip to Durban was uneventful and I spent a couple of weeks buying my stores for the return journey. I also had to find extra horses and wagons which were generally available but often at inflated prices. The supplies were mostly expensive, and I had to walk away from bad deals and hope that the seller was coming after me. I had to remind them that a deal with the British Army was a solemn promise and would not be renegaded upon.

Once again on the road, we made the long journey to catch up with our army. I heard that we had now relieved Ladysmith and the supplies were urgently needed, and I was ordered to get there as fast as I could. Once there, we had to unload quickly and return to Durban for more supplies. My job involved boring journeys over many months, but I did not mind the long days and the deprivation on the road. This was my job and I was pleased to do it to the best of my ability. I knew this was vital support to the British Army and it was my duty to give them the tools to fight and win.

I heard that the war was now coming to an end and the best estimate was a month to victory. However, the Boers were forming small raiding commando groups and frustrating the British and it seemed that the war could carry on indefinitely. Peace negotiations were being carried out as most parties wanted an end to the bloodshed, but a few obstinate Boers wanted otherwise.

When I finally arrived at Ladysmith, I was given a completely new job to do. I was ordered to report to a captain for my orders. He explained that as we had defeated the Boers at recent battles, we now had many thousands of prisoners. We had major problems guarding them and didn't want to see articles and interviews appearing in the world's press about the poor Boer. A decision had been made by the top (that was always a strange way to describe our leaders, I thought) to take the prisoners out of the country. Our prison camps were full and there was always the possibility that the prisoners would be broken out by their own men. We also used prison ships, but they were now full as well. The Boer prisoners were now to be deported to several countries and kept as prisoners until the War was over. I heard later that they were sent to Ceylon, Bermuda and St Helena islands amongst many other places. My job was to take many hundreds of these men to India and to make preparations straight away. I was to report to Captain Cripps who would be in charge of the operation.

We left Durban with almost one thousand men aboard and steamed off towards Calcutta where we arrived a couple of weeks later. I felt sorry for these men who had lost almost everything: families, farms and livelihoods, the war and now their freedom. They were unlikely to return for a year or two and when they did, they would find a different country. They would be lucky to find their families as we learned later that many would die in internment camps, mostly of terrible diseases. These were hard men who had been beaten in every way and their misfortune showed in their faces and their bodies. Their eyes were vacant and empty and their backs bent. They rarely marched with any enthusiasm or energy and I thought that this was cruel and unnecessary humiliation for an enemy already having largely been beaten. I tried to treat the men with kindness and respect and I was tough with my men when they did not do so.

I was amazed once again how young some of them were: many could not yet grow beards and those that did grew huge haystacks of fuzz.

We took detailed information and photographed each man and spent much of the voyage allocating groups of men to prisons of varying sizes. On arrival at Calcutta, we transferred most of the groups on to trains to varying destinations across the country. This was a very complicated logistical exercise, but we were well-trained and experienced for this type of work. At that time, there were around a dozen camps which had been set up in advance.

I took two hundred men to the north of the country and delivered them to five different camps. We even had a small camp near Murree where I had been stationed and it was a good time to catch up with friends. Life for the prisoners was not arduous and they were generally well-fed and kept healthy. Heavy security was not necessary thank goodness and the men were often blended into the local community although they lived separately in communal huts. Many joined local cricket clubs and became experts at the game. There were very few attempts to escape as they would be highly visible and found very quickly.

One of the prisoners did manage to get away: he was in a camp several miles south of Murree where I had left around twenty men. He disguised himself as an Indian and managed to walk many miles and caught a train into French territory where he became a free man. I heard later that he eventually got home to South Africa. He had been one of my prisoners but fortunately, I had handed him over some weeks before!

We got back to Calcutta and the ship was already fully loaded with supplies for our campaign. I was relieved to be leaving as I detested having to look after prisoners in this way and was looking forward to getting back to my real job.

****

The end of a long day was looming, and I was looking forward to a good nights' rest. Firstly, I could rely on our cook for a tasty nourishing meal of stew and a few cups of strong coffee, not to mention a finger or two of Scotch later. I looked up and saw a column of smoke spiralling upwards probably a couple of miles off the track towards the Drakensberg Mountains. I wondered what could be causing this. I spoke to my havildar and in moments, six of us were riding towards the column. I thought there was probably an innocent cause: a farmer burning his waste or a small bush fire, but the smoke was too thick and heavy for either to be likely. When we got closer, we could see that a whole field of corn was alight, and this was unlikely to be an accident. One of my men pointed to a farmhouse in the distance and we rode towards it. There were a group of men carrying a large piano out of the house with great difficulty. As we got closer, I could see that there were beautiful wood carvings on its panels which must have taken a skilled man many months to complete. A small family was watching the men, an old woman, two younger women and three children huddled together in cold fear. One of the men carried an axe and was preparing to chop up this masterpiece in an apparent act of vandalism. I could see that the men, around twelve of them, were British soldiers. I checked that my men were prepared for a confrontation and I rode ahead to speak to the man with the axe.

"What the hell is going on here?" I shouted. Just then a man emerged from a nearby wagon and walked towards me. I could see he was an officer but of a junior rank to me.

"We are just carrying out orders, sir."

"What kind of orders compel you to destroy a piano and herd people out of their houses."

"We are destroying the homes and farms of the Boers to starve them out and force their surrender."

"And is looting part of your orders"

"We are not looting, sir."

"Don't lie to me. I can see your men carrying a clock and cutlery with an obvious intent to steal. I order you to carry the piano and the valuables back into the house and then allow these farmers to return."

The man approached me and said, "Can I show you my orders, sir. They are quite clear." He pulled out a folded paper from his breast pocket and held it out towards me. I took a couple of minutes to read it and was horrified to discover the men were mostly acting in accordance with their orders.

"It says nothing about looting."

"It says that we must destroy these farms and remove the people. We have to destroy the crops and shoot the livestock. You must know that this is going on all over the country."

"I know nothing of the sort and I don't believe you. This is absolutely barbarous."

I was beginning to feel uneasy. Could this possibly be true? I just couldn't believe that British soldiers regularly plundered and looted the poor Boer farmers across the country and destroyed their living. All I had come to believe about my countrymen was beginning to falter and I felt quite shocked.

"You can see that it's authorised by Kitchener himself."

He answered this rather smugly as if this now ended our conversation. I wasn't having this but wanted to find out more.

"What is to happen to the women and children? Where are you taking them?"

I was beginning to dread his answers.

"We have set up huge camps where they are kept together until the surrender comes."

"And the men?" I asked.

"They are being imprisoned separately and many will be deported."

At least I knew this was correct as I had been involved in this.

"So, what happens to their houses?" I already knew the answer.

"We burn them, sir." I wondered just then if the orders were faked so that these men could loot the valuables from the Boers. I could not believe that our British leaders could endorse such an outrageous strategy. I certainly hadn't heard of this before so maybe this was made up. But then again, I had been out of contact for a few months. I wondered if this man was right and I was now living in different place from the one I left before, and I felt dizzy with disbelief and horror. But surely this had to be wrong. I thought quickly and then made up my mind.

"Take the valuables and the piano back into the house and when you have done that let the people back in. You can also draw water from the well and try to put that fire out. There is to be no more looting and destruction. I will shoot anyone disobeying this. And leave those poor animals alone." There were a couple of cows and horses nearby.

"I can't do that, sir. I would be disobeying orders."

I touched the flanks of my horse and moved forward. I pointed my pistol at the officer. "Do it now or I will shoot you."

He reluctantly ordered his men to take the valuables back into the house. He snarled at me with tangible hatred. There was no doubt in my mind that he had been looting.

"And now let these women and children back in."

Just then a shot rang out and one of his men screamed and grabbed his leg as he writhed on the ground.

"That bastard shot me," he shouted pointing at one of my men who had just shot him.

"Havildar, what is happening?" I called out.

"It's all right, sir. That man there drew a gun and tried to shoot you. We shot him first."

"This is mutinous!" the officer shouted. "You will be hanged for this."

"I don't think so. I will recommend that you are demoted, deported and imprisoned when you get back. Your behaviour is outrageous, illegal and criminal. Now, do as I order or more of your men will be shot. Help that man on to the wagon," I said in a calm voice.

He meekly obeyed but I could tell he was seething.

"I will report you when I get back and I don't fancy your chances," he spat these words out with venom.

"Just do what I ordered you to do and get your ugly backsides out of here. You're a bunch of thieves and vagabonds."

In five minutes, they had restored the farmhouse and the women and children went back in. I reminded the men to put the fire out. This was not so easy, and they worked hard for several hours until it was dark. Eventually, we watched them move away in the direction we were headed. I led my men back to our camp for a good meal and sleep. I was rather apprehensive about the outcome of this and had a bad feeling that these men were obeying orders. But how could looting be sanctioned? And how could we British treat men and women so outrageously? Yes, I had been away for several months, but I was sure that we had not altered our moral values to this extent.

When I saw the group of riders and a wagon approaching us from the direction of Ladysmith a couple of days later, I had no doubt what their mission was.

"We have orders to arrest Lieutenant Messenger and an Indian man, the man who shot a British soldier."

"I am Lieutenant Messenger. I am unarmed and will not resist. What are the charges?"

"You will hear all of them later. The main charge is the attempted murder of a British soldier whilst he was going about his legitimate business."

There was absolutely no point in arguing or asking questions. With that I dismounted and walked towards the officer leading the group.

"The man you also want is Sepoy Ganesh. Here he is."

I was surrounded by the men and handcuffed and helped on to my horse. Ganesh was taken into the wagon. I feared for his treatment knowing that they would not be kind to him.

Much later, I was sitting alone in an empty schoolroom which had been converted into a temporary prison. No one had been to see me, and I hadn't been offered any food or drink. My first concern was my extreme thirst and I was well aware of the dangers of dehydration. I was expecting to be offered some water before the nightfall, but I didn't see anyone until the morning. I hadn't slept at all.

I knew I had taken the right action and I was confident that any court would support me. What on earth had taken place while I had been away and why hadn't anyone updated me on my return? I had hardly spoken to anyone since my ship docked and within two days, I was back to work and on the road. I did hear that the Boers were targeting the railways now and it was becoming more hazardous to move supplies by rail. Wagons were also being attacked but so far, the Boers were targeting the very large road trains. I had also heard that a general was transporting his private bathroom and kitchen by this method and this had slowed the road trains down to a crawl. This was outrageous and rather demonstrated the poor attitudes of some of our leaders.

I had also been told about the new Blockhouses which had been built alongside railway lines and bridges to protect them. Some of these were brick built and some more temporary structures with barbed wire strung between them to discourage Boer attacks. They were permanently manned and huge areas were now defended. Someone told me that there were eight thousand of these forts. I shuddered to think of how much of our resources had been put into this project.

There had obviously been major changes while I had been away, but I hadn't heard about them all. I could understand that destroying their homes and farms would leave the Boers without shelter, food and horses. This was still extremely cruel and surely couldn't be the general policy approved by the army. Did the newspapers know about this and what about the British public? I always thought the British believed in a sense of fairness and would never support this cruelty and extermination of a people.

If I accepted, despite my disgust and revulsion, that this had actually been our current policy, how on earth could Britain support the burning of crops, the killing of animals and the deportation of women and children? Where did they take these poor people? I was anxious to find out. And how could we possibly support looting of these homesteads? How many of these farms have been looted and destroyed already? It could have been hundreds by now. How many valuables have been taken already? This could amount to a massive theft of the wealth of a nation. I was very keen to find out the extent of this outrage.

I then considered my own situation and it was not looking good. I was still only a young officer, still shy of my twenty-fifth birthday and right at the start of my life and career in the Indian Army. I had great hopes of a sparkling career and eventually returning to England with enough wealth to buy a small piece of land and raise a family. However, I did not want to live in a nation which supported these vile actions. What had happened to the values of the British people and what has caused this national decline? Queen Victoria was still on the throne and despite her great age, she was symbolic of a nation which believed in justice and fairness, or so I had believed up to now.

I was determined not to be part of this but where would I go and what would I do? What was going to happen to me now? Would I be drummed out of the army in disgrace and sent back to England? How could I face my family and the wrath of my father who would be ashamed of me? I could just hear him saying how I had brought dishonour to him and our family. Nothing like this had ever happened to us before, I could hear him say. I don't think I would even be offered a position at his bank now, but I wouldn't accept it if I was.

I wondered what charges would be brought against me. I guess I would be charged with the wounding of one of our soldiers. Would this be seen as attempted murder? Would my sepoy be charged with murder or would I take the full blame? I very much hoped so as I was afraid he would never get a fair trial. At least as an officer I expected to be given every opportunity to defend myself. I finally managed to convince myself that it was no good worrying as I could not change anything in this way. I may have then fallen into a fitful sleep, but I don't think so.

In the morning, a rather aggressive guard brought me a cup of green water which I drank with glee and asked for another. He ignored me. He also brought some cold porridge. I asked him what was going to happen to me, but he turned his back and left the room.

Much later, I got more water and dry bread but no more information. Towards the end of the day, a young officer arrived and sat down opposite me. He was rather a bookish looking chap but very nervous and spoke to me in a stuttering and hesitant voice. He seemed to be out of place and unsure of himself. He clearly didn't want to be here.

"I am your defence council. A court martial will be held in a few days. They are trying to gather the necessary number of officers and a prosecutor. As you can imagine, the availability of officers is difficult at the moment. Not many are free. They are busy sorting the new administration of Ladysmith and controlling the terrorism of the Boers. Lately, they have been worse than ever and are harrowing our army and support services wherever they can. Then there are thousands of prisoners to look after securely and the camps for the women and children."

I had a hundred questions, but he carried on talking: "As far as I know, these are the four charges you have to answer: attempted murder by one of your men of a soldier of the realm, arming of men of colour contravening the rules of this campaign which apply to both sides, preventing an officer and his men from doing their clear and written duty and threatening a British officer with armed weapons."

"But this is clearly ridiculous. We only wounded the man, and this was in self-defence. He was about to shoot us. Both sides arm men of colour."

This was the first time I had an opportunity to comment but this had little effect on him.

"I think you should accept these charges, admit them and hope for mercy from the Court."

"I absolutely disagree. I will not admit to any of this as I am not guilty."

"Nevertheless, I don't think you have any other choice. I am appointed by the Court and my strong recommendation is for you to admit this and hope for the best. You have no choice in this matter."

I could not believe I was hearing this. What was the point of having a defence counsel when he was not interested in defending me but just wanted to appease the Court? It was no use talking to him.

"I want to appeal this and choose my own defence counsel."

"Sorry, you can't. I have been appointed. I have given you the benefit of my advice and if you don't want to accept this, I can't help you. I will let you know when the first session starts."

I only had to wait two more days.

I looked around the courtroom. The president of the court was a colonel I didn't know. In addition, there were five officers and I had learnt that this was the minimum number required plus a rather nasty looking prosecuting lawyer. He was tall and thin with eyes too close together for my liking. He obviously didn't like me and was only interested in winning the case and with my defence chap supporting him, I had little chance.

"…I, therefore, have no hesitation in recommending to the Court that the accused should face a firing squad for these terrible crimes. At the very least, he should be cashiered from the army and sent back to Britain to serve a long prison sentence. However, I think the former sentence would be the most appropriate."

I am sure you do, I thought to myself, you slimy little bastard. Was he the new kind of Briton without values and decency? No one had bothered to mention my army record which had been exemplary so far—or so I thought.

"This is not the first time that the lieutenant has been in trouble. He disobeyed orders at the battle of Spion Kop," one of the officers added.

I then spoke out. "I helped to save many lives by taking much needed water up to our beleaguered men exposed at the top of the mountain on two occasions. While it was mentioned that I had not been asked to do this, it seemed to be the most appropriate action at the time."

"You should only speak through your defence counsel," the president reminded me.

"I don't want this counsel and anyway, the man appointed," I said nodding towards him, "has no interest or wish to try to defend me. He wants a guilty verdict just as much as the prosecutor does. I wish to appoint my own defence counsel."

"I don't think anyone would want the job under the circumstances," my defence counsel added.

"I demand the right to have a defence counsel of my choosing, someone who recognises that his job is to fight my corner."

I had no idea if I could do this, but it seemed fair and reasonable.

"Also, I demand the right to be fed and watered properly in the meantime. Some days, I am fed nothing at all. I have a right to reasonable food and drink. I haven't been convicted of anything yet, but I am still entitled to eat."

The chairman reminded the Court and therefore me that food and resources were in short supply in Ladysmith. Yes, I thought—I bet you eat and drink well—your pompous bastard.

"I suppose that a change would mean a delay in proceedings which none of us can afford. I will allow a little more time, but you must understand we are all busy people," the chairman kindly reminded us. To me that meant that they have already decided I was guilty and I shouldn't take up any more of their valuable time.

"As far as your living arrangements are concerned—Frederick—would you please look into this," he said nodding to a junior offer at the end of the table.

"I think we should adjourn for now. Gentlemen, are you free to resume next Thursday week?"

As I was led back to my cell, I had a chance to reflect on the proceedings today and I became exceedingly depressed. At least they were giving me an opportunity to change my defence, but I had absolutely no idea how to go about this. I was concerned that they didn't really seem interested in my side of events. They just wanted to convict me and get this over with. On a positive note, I appeared to have batted away the accusation over Spion Kop. Where did that come from anyway? That brigadier must have added my alleged misdemeanour to my army record. I felt resigned to my fate: would they really shoot me for my alleged crimes? I received no food or water again despite the promise to take this up. I had another very bad night.

The following morning, a new guard brought me a flagon of water, strong coffee and some ham and eggs. I can't express how good that was and how much my spirits were lifted. This was a new guard and he was quite pleasant to me. I asked him if I could see the chaplain.

The following day, an elderly man came to see me wearing a dog collar. I was amazed and delighted that at last someone was now looking out for me. He asked me my story and whether he could perform mass for me. I politely declined but my story came spilling out and I raged at the injustice of it all. I told him that I had sacked my defence counsel and needed to replace him with someone who would try a bit harder.

"While you are here, can I ask you a few questions about what has been going on here while I have been away?" He nodded.

"Why are we destroying Boer farms?"

"The strategy is to starve the Boer rebels into submission. We are destroying their sources of food and shelter."

"And as a man of God, do you support this?" I asked.

"No, of course, I don't but I can't do anything about it. I can't go against the commanders of our army as I would lose my commission and position. At least I am in a position to give succour and support to my men. There are far too few of us doing this."

"How many farms have been destroyed?" I asked.

"I hear around thirty thousand farms."

"I just can't believe this. This is extermination of a people. How can British people carry out this outrage?"

"Yes, I agree totally and hate what we are doing but there seems to be no other way to force the Boers to the peace table," he said.

"What is happening to all the women and children they are taking away?"

"They are putting them into vast camps, known as concentration camps. Unfortunately, there have been terrible outbreaks of diseases which have spread like a forest fire. The number of deaths has been huge. These poor people have no immunity to diseases as they haven't been exposed to any in the countryside. It's only the town and city people who have built up immunity. I don't think the authorities considered this when they decided on this policy."

Two days later, just one day before the trial was due to resume, a young officer called in to see me. He introduced himself as Lieutenant Edmund Manwaring-White of the Ox and Bucks Regiment. He had been in South Africa for a couple of years serving under Buller and had been involved in fierce fighting in a dozen engagements. He was tall and slim, about my age, and greeted me enthusiastically. I was impressed with his energy, enthusiasm and friendliness and of course with his magnificent moustache which was still in its infancy. He was funny and engaging and I took to him immediately and asked him why he had come to see me. He told me he had been an articled clerk serving under Sir Roger Oppenheimer, a leading barrister in Lincoln's Inn Field. He was very confident that he could help me, at least save me from the firing squad, and perhaps even my commission.

He had a few days off in Ladysmith and the chaplain of his regiment had approached him after hearing about my situation. He asked a hundred questions about me, my record and about the circumstances which led to my arrest. He also wanted to know about the incident at Spion Kop in case it came up again, although he didn't think it would. I asked him how he was planning to defend me, but he wouldn't give any details. All he said was that he would bring a clerk in with him to take careful notes, even though there was an official recorder. He told me to keep my mouth shut unless he allowed me to speak. He would answer for me when questions were asked. He took many notes and then tidied up his papers, stood up and said he was leaving now to do the hard work. If he needed to speak to me again, it would probably be in the early morning before the court resumed. This was all a huge tonic to me and my morale surged.

He called in very early the next morning and told me he had checked all the officers on the board: he was concerned about the president who was named Lt Col Charles Townshend. He had a brilliant military reputation, but he was well known for his constant lobbying of generals and politicians for his personal advancement and his attempts to smear the reputation of others. Edmund was concerned that he would use this opportunity to further his reputation as a strong decision maker and disciplinarian—all to our disadvantage. He would be watching him and listening carefully. He had a few minor concerns about some of the others, but he saw Townshend as a real threat to our case.

We were soon back in court. I looked at Townshend and tried to identify the others. Soon, the prosecutor was on his feet.

"Gentlemen, I believe I have presented a thorough case: four charges have been brought against Lieutenant Messenger, the most serious being that of attempted murder of a British soldier. For this alone is serious enough for him to face the firing squad, I don't think I need to bore the Court with the other charges. I say guilty on all four counts. Let's show all soldiers that they can't take the law into their own hands without the most serious penalty," concluded the reptilian prosecutor. I nicknamed him the lizard!

Up to now, Edmund had said nothing. He just looked thoughtful, murmured very softly and wrote some notes down on a small pad of paper.

The chairman said, "Are you the defence counsel? If so, please introduce yourself to the Court and explain your credentials to us."

"I am Lieutenant Edmund Manwaring-White of the Ox and Bucks Regiment and I have been engaged in this war for a couple of years. I am here to defend Lieutenant Messenger against these outrageous charges which I believe have been concocted rather more for political reasons than for serious wrongdoing. I have two years' experience as an articled clerk working under Sir Roger Oppenheimer of Lincoln's Inn whom I am sure needs no introduction to you nor further explanation."

I heard an acquiescent murmur from the chairman and a couple of others.

"I decided I would be more usefully employed serving my country overseas, furthering and defending our empire rather than staying at home pursuing litigation cases. I was assured that I would be welcomed back to his chambers when our hour of need was over."

Once again, a soft murmur of approval.

"However, when I heard of my fellow officer's predicament and having a few free days of rest, I had no hesitation in putting forward my services which were gratefully accepted. It was quite manifest that the previous incumbent was totally unsuitable and had no interest in serving the falsely accused."

This time, there was a low growl of disapproval.

"I should, at this stage, introduce my clerk to the Court. His name is Bill Jenkins and his sole duty is to take notes on my behalf."

As he spoke, Bill was busy scribbling.

"To continue: the most serious charge levied at Lieutenant Messenger was the attempted murder of a soldier of the realm: this was not attempted murder, but self-defence carried out by a sepoy. I will bring forward witnesses to demonstrate this and explain events as they happened. If the sepoy had not taken quick and firm action, several soldiers of ours would have been shot and possibly killed. It was very brave of the sepoy to protect and defend the officers and men and it was extremely fortunate that he took positive and swift action. I hope the Court will join me in thanking Sepoy Ganesh for his selfless, prompt and courageous action."

As I expected, there were frosty stares and silence.

"Where is Sepoy Ganesh by the way? I am sure the Court will wish to know that he is well and suitable decorations are being arranged for him."

This time, the chairman of the court could not hold himself back: "He is a potential killer and not a member of our army and will, therefore, not be receiving any recognition. On the contrary, he will have to await his punishment."

"That is regrettable as I have demonstrated that he has behaved like a hero. However, it was his initiative and not that of the officer here present. In other words, he was acting on his own volition. And it's an excellent job that he did because there could have been loss of life if the soldier had been allowed to fire on Lieutenant Messenger's men. As I have said, Sepoy Ganesh deserves our grateful thanks."

He paused to let the Court absorb this point.

"Lieutenant Messenger has no case to answer here. He did not fire a gun and he did not order a gun to be fired. Therefore, this charge is irrelevant."

Again, there was a solid silence.

"This brings me on to the next charge: that this officer armed his native men in contravention of the rules of engagement which apply to both sides and was agreed before the outset of engagement."

I saw several heads nodding in agreement that this rule had indeed been broken. He continued, "I would, therefore, ask this court to summon Colonel Baden-Powell. He has broken this rule many hundreds, if not thousands, of times. And he's not the only one. Every general and commander has broken this rule and not just on our side. Bring Botha here if you can. He and all his commanders are the biggest culprits. I see no reason for a lowly lieutenant not to follow his leaders' actions. I, therefore, demand that this charge is dropped forthwith."

He paused after this and was met with stony glares. The officers were staring at different points of the room in the hope that they would not be asked to respond to this overwhelming argument. It occurred to me again that I was indeed fortunate to have Edmund on my side.

"Can I address the third charge now: that of preventing an officer and his men from doing their clear and written duty? Since when has it been the duty of an officer of the British Army to allow his soldiers to loot valuables from peoples' homes, from innocent women and children? In fact, for looting—read stealing. Where is it written that soldiers are permitted to steal from residents of this country?"

"Colonel, are you aware of this paper?" Edmund asked addressing the chairman.

"Have you read this paper? Where does it say that soldiers can steal from the population? Where does it say they can destroy a piano? I can understand why we might want to destroy crops and sources of food so that we can starve the Boer into submission, but a piano? What harm can a piano do—strike all the wrong notes?"

I heard a muffled giggle from one of the junior officers which was immediately silenced by a frosty glare from the chairman.

"I put it to the Court that these men were not acting as soldiers, as our soldiers, as decent and honourable soldiers of our British Army are expected to act, but as an uncontrolled rabble, an undisciplined mob disobeying orders, not following them and not following their duty and written instructions. They were acting like gutter criminals. We are all here serving as officers of the greatest army of the most powerful country on earth, led by Her Majesty Queen Victoria, the most magnificent monarch the world has ever witnessed. Yet, we allow criminality in our own ranks and to cover up these heinous crimes, we pass the blame on to one of our own exemplary officers."

Again, Edmund paused to let this sink in. Was Edmund being too dramatic? I was rather afraid he was exaggerating the situation somewhat, but I needn't have worried. Looking around the table, his words certainly seemed to be having the desired effect.

"Therefore, it was the duty of this proper and decent officer, Lieutenant Messenger, to prevent unlawful and hooligan behaviour which is inflicting devastating pain and suffering to innocent bystanders of this war. By his courageous actions, he did indeed bring justice to this one family and he should be applauded. If you can defend the actions of these criminal soldiers please speak now: if you can't please keep silent and drop this ridiculous charge."

There was another stony silence. Several faces had reddened in frustration, humiliation and anger. The tension was like a taught string which I sensed was about to snap. It was difficult to define all the emotions which were swirling around the courtroom.

Edmund continued, "I, therefore, would like confirmation that this charge has been dropped and will be deleted from the official sheet."

The court recorder looked nervously around the room for confirmation and receiving none, made the appropriate notes in his book.

"Please confirm this has been done. A nod will do for now." The Recorder half-nodded in a quick nervous movement.

"The third and fourth charges are closely linked to the second one and again, I assume they will be struck off also."

"No, they bloody well won't! This is an outrage. As far as I am concerned, there are still extremely serious charges to be faced. I refuse to have any struck off at all." Townshend was furious—so much so that his spittle was spraying over the officers sitting opposite him who subtlety moved aside to avoid getting wet. At least he had the balls to confront Edmund— though against overwhelming arguments.

"You, sir, are a bounder and if I had the power, I would have you horsewhipped. You have been extremely rude to distinguished members of this court. I call for this farce to be terminated now and the accused be executed in the manner described." The prosecutor, seeing that he was about to lose his case, was understandably furious. He said this while turning towards the chairman. After a short pause the chairman said, "This session is over. We will convene at 9 a.m. tomorrow. Gentlemen, if you can please stay behind, we will discuss this.

Please leave us now." He waved condescendingly for the three of us to leave.

Edmund came back with me to the cell. Once we were left alone I gratefully said, "My God, that was brilliant. You really had them rattled."

"Yes, but tomorrow, they will get their revenge. I am sure they will keep to all or at least some of their charges and try to make them stick. It's a good job I have an ace up my sleeve." He would not explain further.

I was keen to understand more of what had been going on while I had been away. I had many questions for Edmund and he patiently brought me up to date.

I felt much better that evening and after a reasonable meal and a large nip of whisky which Edmund had smuggled in to me, I slept like a little child. The court resumed the following day. The chairman opened proceedings.

"We have given further thought to your arguments and have decided to amend the charges. We have introduced a charge of allowing a native to wound a British soldier. That will be the only charge. We will take away your commission," the Chairman was addressing me, "and you will be sent back to England but there will be no further imprisonment. You will, of course, not be allowed back into the British Army, even as a private in the ranks."

I was amazed with Edmund's success in forcing this decision, but he reacted as if he had achieved nothing at all.

"This is completely unacceptable." Edmund reddened in anger and frustration:

"Lieutenant Messenger is a good and exemplary officer and I will not let him be treated like this. This is an absolute disgrace and I refuse to allow his character to be stained in any way whatsoever. This is a disgusting and disgraceful decision and not one I would expect from members of our distinguished British Army and from our great Country. Our Queen, Parliament and people will be horrified when they hear about this. I demand that you reconsider."

Again, I was worried he was going over the top for dramatic effect.

"Absolutely not! You have no choice in this matter as we have made our decision. That is what this court is charged to do.

We have greatly reduced the charges levied and we have in fact spared this man's life. You and he should be extremely grateful for the lenience of this court under these dire circumstances. Now, if you have nothing further to add, and I would strongly recommend a long period of silence from you and a respectful exit. This court martial is over," the chairman concluded.

"Very well," Edmund replied. "Gentlemen—I have not been entirely honest with you," Edmund said slowly with gravitas.

I heard cries of: "I knew it. The man is a fraud!"

Edmund continued, "I introduced Bill Jenkins to you at the start of the proceedings as my clerk and this is not the whole truth. He is in fact Albert Fortescue-Williams who I am sure you know is the African Correspondent for the Times. I am surprised and relieved that you didn't recognise him. He was not taking notes for me—he was in fact writing his column for next Wednesday's edition which he will telegraph to London later today. He has made careful notes of all your names and ranks, and I am sure you will be proud to know he will put them in highlights in his article. You could all be minor celebrities in Britain by this time next week. I am sure also, although I have no influence on what he writes, of course, he will tell about your lies, trumped up charges, criminal actions and cover ups. I am sure the good British public will be pleased to know how brave and principled you all are. They will also want to know about the disgraceful and disgusting way this war is being waged. I am also sure you will want him to record that all charges against Lieutenant Messenger have been dropped and that he will be recommended for promotion and a well-deserved decoration. Before I leave here, I would like written confirmation that all this has been done and finally that Sepoy Ganesh be released without charge."

Edmund concluded, "And that I think, Gentlemen, is the finale of proceedings. Good afternoon to you all."

The three of us left the room with as much dignity as we could. We could see the shock and open-mouthed horror on all those reddening faces and they knew that they had been soundly beaten. I felt dizzy with relief and gratitude as we closed the door on them. The written confirmation was delivered to us in minutes.

"Let's go and have a bloody good drink!" We obeyed Edmund gladly and followed him to a local bar.

We said nothing about the case for about an hour. I was so relieved and grateful to this marvellous man.

"I can't thank you enough for what you have done. And you of course, Albert."

"Albert, my name is not Albert—nor is it Bill. I'm David Pinder. I have lived over here for many years and run a shop in a nearby town."

"But Edmund, you said he was the African Correspondent."

"I lied!" Edmund winked at me as he said this.

"And I suppose you were not even an articled clerk."

"Never ever been to Lincoln's Inn Fields, old chap."

"Then who is this Oppenheimer fellow?"

"Blowed if I know. Not a bloody clue!"

"I think it's my round now," I said.

I have never slept as well as I did that night.

The Wilderness of Zin:
Eddie's Venture into Sinai

Not where the squadrons mass,
Not where the bayonets shine,
Not where the big shell shout as they pass
Over the firing-line;
Not where the wounded are,
Not where the nations die,
Killed in the cleanly game of war—
That is no place for a spy!
O Princes, Thrones and Powers, your work is less than ours—
Here is no place for a spy!

Rudyard Kipling

The worst bit was crossing that huge desert area, so enormous
that you felt insignificant in the vast sea of sand which went on
forever. When I had the energy to think, which was getting more
difficult, it reminded me of that wonderful William Blake poem,
To See a World in a Grain of Sand, but most of the time, I was
too tired to focus beyond the moment and for the next swig of
water. We had to ration the water to a bottle a day—very tough
indeed—when ten bottles would not have been enough. It's
strange though that you can train yourself to drink less water by
reducing the amount every day. You can also train horses to
drink less in this way. Above us hung a golden sun in a huge blue
sky and it dazzled and disorientated me.

Our group, with a dozen Bedouins on camels and horses,
crept and skidded across the desert from dune to dune like an
army of ants. The stark colours of the desert sand and the
changing light and sun burnt into my eyes and filled my head. A
soft wind swept over us and quickly became hot and suffocating

as its strength increased: the Arabs had often talked about the desert wind, the khamsin and its destructive power and soon, it became a near gale. The sand was driven into our faces, into our eyes making them gritty, opening wounds around our noses and mouths. I turned around to see how my neighbours were protecting themselves. I pulled my headcloth over my nose and my head cover down leaving a narrow slit to see my way forward but still my existence was intolerable.

I fleetingly remembered putting my hand into my mother's oven once and then pulling it out quickly. The heat was almost like that and it near broiled my whole body. The heat and the glare made me so dizzy and then the sky and the sun started spinning and crashing down on me. The effect made me physically sick and I spat out the result. I wondered how anyone could survive this on-going torture. I looked around and the Bedouins were probably suffering nearly as much as me but were stoically facing the elements with grim expressions. They knew what to expect having crossed a hundred deserts and I am sure it never got any easier. I thought back to my childhood and my easy time at school when I loved to read about the exploits of soldiers and explorers when they crossed thousands of miles of Eastern lands and faced all manner of obstacles and they overcame each one with British grit.

I now realised that I was not like them, not made of the same mettle and I really should not have come here. My body could not cope with these elements: I wished I was back in our own temperate climate which my body was made for. I then remembered the thousands of our men who had no choice but to endure hardships in many parts of the southern world and I shook myself physically and mentally and became a man again for a short time. I looked across at Ned and that chap always amazed me.

Ned Lawrence was one of the two archaeologists in our party. Nothing seemed to faze him, and he had endured some terrible weathers and hardships without even flinching. I had heard about his incredible stamina and long, long tough journeys which he completed without a whimper and indeed got down to work as soon as he arrived at his destination. He must have survived a thousand days and journeys like this one. How the hell did he do it? He seemed to be tougher than all of them. His stamina and courage impressed even his Arab friends: it must be mental toughness that he and people like him possessed. I was sure that I didn't have this ability but now, I was being severely tested as surely things couldn't be harder than this. And then came the tiredness.

Mile after mile, we trekked on and my head was nodding in unison with my camel. I dropped off to sleep and then awoke with a sudden jerk. And then I nodded off again. Ned saw my situation and yelled across at me:

"Eddie—splash your head and face and the back of your neck with a little water and then get off your camel and walk for a mile."

I obeyed and kept going for a while. After walking for two thousand paces, I then had difficulty getting back on my camel and when I did, I nodded off again. My camel stopped, and I beat its rump to move on, but he knew I was going to nod off again and then he could have another rest. After several repeats, I could see that the others had overtaken me and in moments, I was being left behind. Ned did not notice me this time and I fell into a deep sleep. Awaking once more, I tapped my beast's behind a bit harder and he moved forward reluctantly with a jerking movement. Then the pattern was repeated and then I couldn't remember anything at all.

Several hours later, I was dimly aware of lying in a tent. An Arab reported to Ned that I had nodded off again and disappeared. They both guessed I had fallen off the camel, crashed to the ground and lay there unable to move. Ned had found me and strapped me across the camel so that I could not fall again. He walked the camel back to the camp while I was unconscious on top. It was a journey of many miles, many extra miles for him in a day which was already too long, and night had fallen. Ned realised I was seriously ill and he ordered an Arab to look after me and tend to my needs. I was unconscious for many days and by the time I awoke, I could not talk or move. My carer had fed me water but could not get me to eat. I was now so weak that I knew I was dying. Ned later said that there were dozens of poisonous snakes all around me when he eventually found me after several hours.

The Arabs bathed my body and let me take sips of water to try to regain my body moisture. They let me sleep for a day and a night and then woke me to drink some more. They told me that my body was badly dehydrated and that I was suffering from heatstroke. I also had hugely painful sores from the constant rubbing of the camel saddle. I really needed a prolonged period of rest, but we could not afford the time and I dreaded being responsible for holding the venture up. They let me have one more day of rest and then I painfully climbed back on to the back of a different camel. I felt slightly better now and after a few days, I was fitter and stronger than before and was very careful to protect myself against the strong sun and to drink enough water. I was just beginning to acclimatise. Fortunately, the deadly khamsin had blown over and the air was now still.

Our Bedouin guide kept a watchful eye on me saying, "Our desert is not a good place for you white skinned Englishmen. Even we find the elements challenging and we were born to this."

I still found that the heat was unbelievable, and I was the only one of our group new to this. My English colleagues were browned and scarred from the sun and the heat from a thousand days. I had spent years in India and South Africa, but nothing had prepared me for this intensity. We had some hard work to do each day when all I wanted to do was rest under cover.

I had been in Army Intelligence for a couple of years now and I was based in Cairo. I had had plenty of adventures since my first experience of conflict in South Africa. I had been posted to India twice, London twice and East Africa once and this was my second outing in Sinai. I was now a Captain and I had just reported back to the Cairo office for my next assignment. I was now a married man, and this had shocked my old friends. They could not believe that the romping old soldier had now been tied down—finally. Molly and I were married at St Mary's, Mendlesham. She had changed her name from Lavinia Wilhelmina Van Toll to Molly Manwaring-White whilst I had not changed at all, well not my name anyway.

Molly was lovely and loving and was related to Dutch royalty: but that is not what attracted me to her: as soon as I first saw her—in a casino in London—I knew she was special. I was on a long losing streak and I was just leaving the table when she sat in the vacant chair opposite me. I sat down again quickly. She was very cool and confident and obviously knew her way around a poker table and she was not at all daunted to be playing with six leery old men. I watched her play with considerable skill and calmness: she was ahead immediately and then began to lose ground. She must have been thirty pounds down when she began to gain again slowly. After around an hour, which seemed to speed by in minutes, she was ahead but not by much. Slowly, she improved and then three of the men threw their cards down and in the final game, she must have been a hundred up. She left the table and I threw my cards in—I hadn't had a good run—and I stood up to follow her as she made her way towards the restaurant.

"Excuse me," I called out to her. "Would you care to join me for a bite?"

"You were at the table, weren't you? Have you got enough money left?"

I thought that was a bit cheeky but kept my cool—after all I was very experienced with women and these kinds of occasions.

"Just about enough for a whisky and maybe then a plate of smoked salmon."

As we spoke, it took only a few moments to fall under her charm and I must admit that I was quickly smitten. A couple of days later, I burned my black book and had the difficult job of persuading my currently lady friend to vacate my flat. There were screams and threats but eventually, I won the day. I decided that Molly was the one for me even though at the time she was not so sure. She didn't make the going easy for me and each time we met, it was rather like I was meeting her for the first time. Just when I thought I was getting somewhere, she would put me down, but in a nice fun way. She was extremely unimpressed with my career and with the stories I told constantly, at least she pretended to be but always left me unsure. She became a constant challenge for me and I found her to be irresistible.

Molly was always extremely well-dressed, of medium height, full-bodied as one would say and had a natural poise which always fascinated me. She spoke beautiful English with a trace of an endearing Dutch accent. When she walked, all male eyes in a room locked on and followed her. I would describe her as a real lady. After months of courting, she invited me to her family home in Alkmaar where I was examined carefully by many members of her family. She had been married before to a Scotsman called McIntosh but was now divorced and she didn't keep his name. I never knew anything about him and she wouldn't mention him any further. She had lived in London for a couple of years now and worked in the Dutch diplomatic corps. I was never quite sure exactly what her job was, but I knew that my Molly was a very clever lady and fully wrapped up in her work.

A week later, I travelled to Egypt and it was another year before I saw her again back in London. This time, it was her turn to meet my father, the rector and my devoted mother. We were married within weeks but unfortunately, I had to return to Egypt. It was agonising to leave her behind.

We were close to the Palestinian coast now near Gaza and could see evidence of increased Turkish security in the area. The guards marched up and down in front of us looking nervous. Their fingers were half squeezing the triggers on their rifles. They seemed to be suspicious of us and our presence here, but we had good cover with our two well-known archaeologists who were always busy looking for evidence of the past. While the landscape seemed, to our uneducated minds, to be sterile and sun burnt, to them they saw the riches of earlier times and peoples.

Today, they were excitedly dancing around an innocuous pile of stones and talking in high voices. Even in the most barren places they found cairns, stone circles and piles and assured us these were either burial mounds or places of earlier worship. They would take hundreds of photographs, often with one of us standing close to give scale. They talked in excited voices, taking copious notes and drawing with crayons on large sketch pads. Where the hell did they get their energy from? I just wanted to curl up into a foetus position under cover of my canvas. I just didn't have their enthusiasm and strength. But I had to pretend to demonstrate my involvement and expertise. We were all dressed in flowing Arab robes which helped to keep us cool and clean. Western clothes would have been extremely uncomfortable in this fierce heat.

Many times, during the weeks of our trip, Turkish guards would come to us pointing their guns and demanding in broken English to know what we were doing in this wilderness and what we could possibly find interesting in this burnt desert. They constantly asked for our papers and proof that we really were doing what we said we were. Of course, our archaeologists had acres of papers which they patiently and slowly read aloud and showed more photographs and drawings than the men were interested in. They soon got bored and gradually would drift away from us eccentric Englishmen and leave us in peace.

Our cover was working well: whilst we had two genuine archaeologists with us, we also had two military men and several Arab servants. The main purpose of our visit to the Sinai Peninsula was two-fold: one was to assess the current levels of Ottoman strength with evidence of fortifications and armaments. The other was to gain topographical knowledge so that our army could plan their future operations. We had to make detailed maps of the land and this was my area of expertise. We had been commissioned by Kitchener as he and many others were sure that the Turks would try to hold the Suez Canal and prevent our vital access through there in the event of war.

Most people believed that war was imminent, and Kitchener was determined to be well prepared and to plan routes and strategies for our army. He wrote to the archaeologists at the huge dig at Carchemish asking them to carry out a survey of this region and Newcombe, that is Captain Stewart Newcombe and I pretended to assist them whilst in reality we were looking for military evidence—and we found plenty in the six weeks we spent in the area. Captain Newcombe was an experienced officer of the Royal Engineers and although we were of equal rank, he was senior to me on this venture. This was never a problem as we got on famously—in fact he was popular with all the team. I had some military intelligence experience whilst stationed in Cairo over the past few months and now, I had a practical exercise to carry out. We brought the briefing letter from Kitchener to Carchemish and discussed the plan with the two men.

As I mentioned before, I found it to be extremely tough to keep up with these men and their Arab servants, all hardened by the desert suns for many years. And indeed, they were used to sleeping through the frosty nights and the frequent rain in this winter season. During one spell, we had intense rain for three days and nights which pleased the Arabs, not for the cold and wet which they hated, but for the knowledge that corn, and vegetables would be in abundance this year. This was not always the case in his part of the world.

The Arab servants looked after us well and provided plenty of water and good provisions for us. I loved the rich coffee they made in the mornings and evenings. They carried all these provisions on bloody-minded camels and indeed this was our main method of transport.

Most of the land was dry and dusty with craggy rocks and high mountains and the traces of riches of the past held only a middling interest for me—well certainly in the early weeks anyway. However, during the long cool evenings after our stew cooked over an open fire, our archaeologists spoke of their love of the past and the precious land we were now in. They explained that we were following in the path of the great Exodus where the Israelites had escaped out of Egypt after their many years of slavery. The leading archaeologist was Leonard Woolley and he had been working with Ned Lawrence as his assistant for several months at the Carchemish site. Ned had a mesmerising voice and could hold an audience for hours. He ignited an interest in us about the long, incredible history of these peoples and the leadership of Moses who took them on a long road to the promised land over a period of forty years. He was also an expert map maker.

"In a few days' time, we will experience the magnificence of the Mount Sinai where Moses climbed to find God and bring his message back to the people. We will also view the honeyed walls of St Catherine's monastery in the foot of the mountains where the *Syriac Sinaitic*, a translation into Syriac of the four canonical gospels, and the *Codex Sinaiticus*, a handwritten copy of the Greek Bible, was held for many years and is now in the safekeeping of the British Library. This is a where some of the world's most beautiful icons are looked after. My favourite is *The Ladder of Divine Ascent*, which pictures monks climbing up to Jesus on a ladder whilst demons fire arrows at them. But nothing compares to the majesty of the huge mountain overwhelming the monastery. In your imagination, you can see Moses climbing up the huge and steep sides to meet with God until he descended clutching His laws deeply etched on tablets of stone."

This was one of many interesting lectures which Ned gave. We never got bored with all his fascinating detail. Ultimately, we could only spend a couple of hours at the monastery, but I was determined to return someday.

We asked plenty of questions and he answered them all enthusiastically with incredible knowledge. Ned was an extraordinary character who had almost a spiritual presence. He was the shortest man in our party—in fact he was not a lot over five foot—and was aware and rather embarrassed that his head seemed too big for his body. He would not join us each evening with our tasty stews as he stuck to a strict vegetarian diet. His close companion, Dahoum, used to prepare vegetarian dishes for both. He avoided alcohol and tobacco also—unlike the rest of us who probably enjoyed both rather too much.

Whist he was extremely good company, he told us that he had little respect for officers (ourselves excluded, he added charmingly) and had always taken pride in disobeying them. He avoided wearing uniform, he was not currently required to, but when he did, he managed to look rather scruffy and unsmart.

Ned often talked about his first visit to this magical part of the world when he walked to thirty-seven crusader castles covering some eleven hundred miles over several months. He was badly beaten and almost killed during his journey. He had also cycled the length and breadth of France and Britain looking at the architecture of old castles and churches. His thesis at Oxford was the comparison of western and eastern castle styles. He earned an outstanding degree being in the unusual situation of knowing far more about the subject than anyone alive including his examiners. We never tired of his stories which kept us up late at night. He was as popular with us as he was with our accompanying Arabs. He seemed to blend in and become one of them.

Woolley told us that Ned loved high speeds and when not cycling, had several motorbikes. Whilst at Carchemish, he had a powerful motor sent to him from England which he had attached to the back of a boat and enjoyed hair-raising jaunts along the Euphrates.

I noticed that Ned increasingly liked to be called T E using his first two initials. He often talked about his destiny and I had no doubt that he would find his mission in life. He had the intelligence, energy and as he said he often dreamed by day which made him one of the world's dangerous men. I was sure that his future lay in this part of the world. In time, of course, he would be known to the world as Lawrence of Arabia.

Meanwhile, Woolley and I took careful notes of the military strength of the region and topographical details and invented a code only understood by us when challenged by suspicious soldiers.

We travelled mainly by camel but when we moved up north, we went by train which was a pleasant relief. On our way, we were able to visit Petra. I had heard so much about this wonderful place, but I was not prepared for its magnificence. It was Ned's first visit as well and while I was overwhelmed with the incredible carving of the Treasury building, he was almost in ecstasy over the colours of the rocks. He took many pictures and drawings but had great difficulty in recording and describing the incredible details to his satisfaction. He spent a couple of hours painting on canvasses trying to faithfully represent the colours, fissures and cracks of the rocks. I was most impressed with his accuracy and passion.

After visiting the interior of the Treasury, which I thought was rather plain and uninteresting, we travelled by camel through the narrow gap of the cliffs, paddling through a stream of spring water. The gap only allowed one camel at a time and I had to be careful to avoid a tap on the head from the overhanging rocks. We had time to visit a few cave homes which had been carved into the rock, but one would need many days to do justice to the vastness of this Nabatean city. I commented to our guide that it must have taken years for a man to carve out a home for his family and was told no, the rock is so soft that this would only take a few weeks. I think I was more impressed by this and the size and quality of these ancient homes than any other aspect of this fabulous city. I felt privileged to have seen the place and I now enjoy entertaining my friends with my experiences of Petra over a few glasses of port after a good dinner.

We needed to return to Carchemish in the north of Syria to finish the dig and we travelled with them, mostly by train and were delighted to learn more about the site and the fantastic history of the great battle and the magnificent King Nebucadrezzar. Ned and Woolley had nearly finished their dig and later, they had decided to return to England to write up their findings.

The Wilderness of Zin by Thomas Edward Lawrence and Leonard Woolley was a masterpiece of the history of the area. I was very proud to have been part of the expedition to this desolate but fascinating part of the world but was also rather pleased that the ordeal was nearly over. These men worked hard in some of the toughest conditions in the world.

Meanwhile, Stewart and I decided to travel to our offices in Cairo as our superiors were very keen to learn our findings. We were also able to report in detail the progress of the Baghdad railway which was being built by the Germans nearby. We had a clear view of site and watched as they used Arab labour to build a vast bridge over the river for the tracks. We were also involved in a riot lead by the Arabs as the Germans had reneged on the agreed payment for their services. We thought that there was going to be mass slaughter and became involved to calm the situation down. The Germans never seemed to learn the wisdom of dealing honestly with the locals.

Shortly after our arrival, I was ordered to return to my regiment in India as I was needed for a major offensive being planned in Mesopotamia. I was disappointed as I was beginning to enjoy this intelligence work which was very different from being an infantry officer.

Before we all left the dig, I questioned the two men about the ancient battle of Carchemish and their findings on this site and I listened with fascination as Ned described the scene.

"The Babylonians had travelled the long journey to the north following the magnificent River Euphrates from City of Babylon. They were led by the mighty warrior Nebuchadnezzar and he was determined to destroy the Egyptian Pharaoh Necho and to claim his wealth and fortune and the lands he had conquered.

"Necho had recently won a mighty battle against the Israelites at Megiddo and he was also keen to increase his wealth and land ownership. He had never been to Babylon but many travellers had told him about its magnificence and he was keen to take control. The Babylonians crossed the Euphrates here at this natural ford and faced the might of the Egyptian Army. Incidentally, we had found plenty of evidence that both sides had mercenaries from nearby countries. We found pottery which suggests that Nebuchadnezzar had hired Grecian charioteers and there is little doubt that Necho had many well-trained soldiers captured from Palestine. Behind me, you can see the line of stones which is all that is left of the mighty fortress of the city where the Syrians hoped to hold against the enemy.

"For many hours, the two massive armies faced each other on open land. There were rows of armoured bowmen, foot soldiers and charioteers, perhaps ten thousand on each side. They spent hours glaring at each other whilst the leaders sent runners to exchange messages to negotiate the future. Could war be avoided by the exchange of land and goods? Was there a way forward to exist together in peace? Hard bargaining took place.

"Whilst this was going on, a noise rumbled across the Babylonian Army and men pointed to the south where small smoking fires were displaying a pre-arranged message. Thousands of these fires had been lit, three every mile, to relay the news from Babylon that the king was dead, and Nebuchadnezzar was now king in the place of his father. This seemed to add an urgency to the Babylonian Army and they were now clamouring for a fight, beating their shiny shields with urgency and belligerence. The horses cried and whinnied with the noise and tension which was like a tangible force. Every man knew that at the end of the battle, if victorious, they would return to their city with their new king in triumph and there would be many days of feasting and revelry at his coronation. They would look forward to this and a fat payment on arrival as a reward for a long and tough campaign.

"The two cavalries charged at each other with increasing speed and clashed together with terrible force and there was an inevitable slaughter of men and horses; then the infantries moved forward stepping over the fallen bodies and heard a thunder of crashing metal. The war engines moved towards the massive castle walls where thousands of the Syrian Army were waiting in anticipation of the attack. These vast machines were rolled on huge metal wheels hauled by horses and oxen and were pulled and pushed by many hundreds of men.

"Slowly, the massive engines creaked forward and after an hour or so covered the few hundred yards to face the walls. Each massive box-like machine contained a huge log trimmed down from the largest cedar tree with an iron tipped point. These logs hung from long ropes and were pushed and pulled backwards and forwards by the men creating massive pressure blows against the twenty-foot-thick walls. Meanwhile, other men climbed up inside the structure until they were facing the enemy along the battlements. Immediately, dozens of men were thrown off the structure by jets of scalding oil aimed at the top platforms of the seven machines.

"The scalding oil was propelled with such devastating force and accuracy that the men were burnt alive. Their screams were truly terrible as they fell to the ground. Sparks caused by the heat created explosions and fires which other men rushed to douse. None of the men survived this onslaught and their broken and burnt bodies covered the ground. They were clearly unprepared for this and it took them several hours to recover and fight back. They had already lost two hundred men. More men were then moved forward and concentrated on swinging back the logs and crashing them into the walls..."

The story Ned told was so vivid and colourful that the land and the walls came alive and the ancient figures danced on the land. Unfortunately, I then fell into a blissfully deep sleep dreaming of ancient battles, deserts and lands.

Political Officer:
Gerald's Work in Mesopotamia

If you can talk with crowds and keep your virtue,
Or walk with Kings—nor lose the common touch,
If neither foes nor loving friends can hurt you,
If all men count with you, but none too much;
If you can fill the unforgiving minute
With sixty seconds' worth of distance run,
Yours is the Earth and everything that's in it,
And—which is more—you'll be a Man, my son!

Rudyard Kipling

Some said I was a cruel man but that is not the way I saw it. I know I have a terrible temper, a very short fuse but that is not the reason I bashed the Arab repeatedly. I needed to show him and his friends who was in charge here and I wasn't to be crossed. The look on the shaik's face confirmed his guilt as far as I was concerned and confirmed the intelligence I had received. The Turks knew everything about my activities behind their lines— even the small details about the network of children who passed me information. I gave them sweets and small sums to get me much needed information and to get them to run errands for me. The ferret-faced Arab looked at me with a hang dog expression and started to deny his involvement, pleading and begging me to believe him, but I didn't. I grabbed him by the shoulders and shook him hard.

"You miserable, lying, Arab bastard. I'm going to teach you a lesson you'll never forget."

I then slapped him hard across his face.

"I want to know the truth from you and I will carry on hurting you till you tell me all. You will be begging me to kill you quickly in just a few minutes."

The truth started to come out between the wailing and tears. He said he was forced to tell all to the Turks under pain of death. I didn't believe him at all. I dragged him out of his house shouting at him in my loud booming voice so that all his friends would know what he had done. I hoped this would deter others and make them think twice before betraying me. I threw him over his horse and tied his hands to his feet below the horse's stomach. To frighten him further, I blindfolded him and as we rode out of the village, I had a good audience from dozens of his friends who stood silently outside their houses. We rode to Basra where I dumped him in a side street still wearing his blindfold and I didn't drop him gently to the hard floor. He knew that he was lucky to be alive and would not forget this and of course neither would his friends.

I had started to build up a formidable reputation and a network of people loyal to me and more importantly, to Britain and India. On another occasion, I took a miscreant back to his people and shot him dead in front of his friends. I didn't hear a murmur as they all understood that he had betrayed my trust and theirs. After this, it was rare for my movements and activities to be reported to the Turks. It was a harsh way to carry on, but I had learned that you had to dominate these people to earn their respect and loyalty. The British rules of fair play did not apply here, and I would have failed much earlier on if I had not been very tough with the locals who crossed me.

Most of the Arab groups were loyal to the Turks and it took me many months of demanding work to try to convert them to our cause. I would follow our army north up the Tigris and learn about their requirements. The men were perpetually hungry, and I would often bring them herds of sheep which I had bought from neighbouring Arabs. Fruit and wheat were very much in demand and I kept the men as well supplied as I could. All men love trade and prompt payment and some local tribes transferred their loyalty to us as a result or at least became neutral. I often travelled by boat on the Tigris and in this way, could move relatively quickly. I became aware of other men like me but working for the enemy. There was a big competition to gain dominance and win hearts and minds.

I had earlier worked along the Euphrates and I was caught up in the fierce battle of Shaiba where I had waded several miles across flood plains. We eventually won the battle, but I was horrified by the numbers of Arab horsemen riding against us and I determined to do something about this. Later, I received permission to return to this area and try to recruit at least some of the locals. I was partially successful but was now required to work further east to support our advancing army. My temporary base was just by old Babylon and it took a little imagination to picture the huge buildings, the hanging gardens, the grand palaces and the myriad of canals criss-crossing the city. This was the Venice of Mesopotamia only much more magnificent than any city before or after. It was tragic to see the city in such decline now.

I was employed as a political officer reporting to my office in Basra and HQ in Cairo. Basra was like a hornet's nest of spies from at least a dozen countries and I spent time drinking and eating in the bars and restaurants to gain information. Once I was surprised to discover that each of the six men in a particularly seedy bar were spies from different countries and each one of them probably knew who I was as well! I returned to Basra quite often to report news and to get orders and to gain valuable intelligence.

I nearly always dressed in Arab clothes and went months without a proper wash. With my dirty looks and language skills, I was always taken for a local, even by my own people. This suited me perfectly well and I had spent many hours and days learning the several languages and accents of the region. I had so often been struck with all kinds of diseases and severe hardships but rarely had the luxury of nurses, medicines and recovery time and had to carry on and sweat my way through. Consequently, I was thin and skinny, and my skin was a rather unhealthy yellowy brown which helped with my disguise somewhat.

Our army was having remarkable success and advancing rapidly north towards Baghdad and it seemed that nothing would stop them. With our disaster at the Dardanelles, it became politically important in London and India to take Baghdad and for a time, it seemed that nothing would stop us. I continued my work getting much needed supplies for the army from my Arab contacts. The supply from Basra up the Tigris was pitiful and impeded the performance of our men and so my help was needed more than ever.

My main contact in the army was Eddie, or to give him his full title, Lt Col Edmund Manwaring-White. By extraordinary coincidence, Eddie was my cousin being the son of my father's sister and he and I had always got on well with good understanding. Our views about the war and situation were in harmony. Eddie constantly needed information about the enemy and so much of my work was carried on behind enemy lines. I had established a field-telegraph system to which a group of renegade Arabs had cut and so once again, I carried out swift punishments before the new line was installed.

I needed to get information on enemy numbers, their guns, equipment and shipping and perhaps as importantly, Eddie needed news about their morale, health and supplies. Despite aircraft reconnaissance from the Flying Corps and other sources, he was receiving poor or inaccurate information. I learned that Eddie had worked in Intelligence in Cairo and across the region and so, we shared a mutual respect. On my latest trip to see him, I gave him the bad news about the high numbers of the enemy forces, roughly three times our numbers. To make matters worse, I learned that high calibre troops were coming back from the Dardanelles to strengthen their army.

I worked with a small team of loyal Arabs and we tried to cause havoc behind the enemy lines. We carried out most of our work at night cutting their lines of communication and destroying their arms and shipping. We must have launched more than a dozen raids; after one successful sortie to blow up a munitions store, we were attacked by a large enemy force which had spotted us. Half my men were killed in the first couple of minutes and the six remaining were surrounded and trapped and a fierce shooting match ensued. I thought that this time our luck had run out, but I managed to find a drain under a nearby road and hid in there with two of my men until the enemy gave up and moved on, perhaps thinking that we had all been shot in the melee.

****

That damned Abu dropped his rifle and the clatter, clatter as it bounced off the rocks woke everyone up for miles around until it found a flat place down below. Unfortunately, the bridge was bristling with Turkish soldiers and they were certain to spot us and start firing. Seconds later, bullets were whistling around our ears and crackling off the rocks as we turned and scrambled down the cliff for safety. To make matter worse, Abu threw the dynamite into the river in case a lucky bullet—lucky that is for the Turks—set it off and that would have turned all of us into burnt offerings. I made a mental note to speak to Abu later, although I wouldn't be doing much speaking. But we had to run for our lives as their bright lights made us easy targets. We didn't all make it down safely; five of my men were shot down in that rush for safety and cover. I made a quick calculation that fourteen were now left and hoped that we didn't have wounded to carry. Our chances of survival were slim, and we were many miles behind enemy lines with no supply. The vegetation at the base of the cliff gave us good cover and we ran like demented dervishes as we could hear the soldiers following us. I looked around for a hiding place and cursed when I could find nothing. All we could do was run and run. After about an hour, it seemed that we had shaken them off and we hid in caves in a rock face. I coughed and gasped and slowly got my breath back lying back with great relief. Luckily for Abu, he had been shot during our descent; he would have faced much worse with my anger. I reckoned we had about forty miles to cover to get back to our camels and stores. We had little water and food and the walk would be tough and with the threat of discovery by the enemy, it was another tight spot. I had been in worse though and braced myself for a long slog. To make matters worse, some of my men started to moan and one was limping badly, but we couldn't afford to stop.

The journey gave me a chance to reflect on the past few weeks. My plan had been to blow the Aziz Bridge above the river and to take a train down with it. This would have given the Turks a huge problem and could delay their advance some weeks. It would have been a great coup for us, but we had failed. I was furious with my men and our intelligence but most of all, I was very angry with myself. I should have taken more time to recce the area and would have discovered that the bridge contained hundreds of Turks. Had we been betrayed and if so, who had the opportunity to do this? We needed to have another crack at the train, but I didn't think we had enough dynamite and other essentials and had little opportunity to restock here. We might have to make the long journey back to our lines and I really didn't want to do this. When we finally returned to our base camp, I was relieved to find that we had some dynamite left, just enough to complete the job.

I decided not to go back to the bridge which was too heavily guarded but found an ideal spot in open desert where the train would pass. I planted the dynamite in a culvert just under the rail and then I had just started burying the wire when I heard the train rumbling along in the distance and I saw its mass looming towards me. I saw soldiers poking their guns out of every window. I had no chance of getting this one and I was exposed just yards from the track. I had the opportunity to make a run for it, but I doubted I would make it. I was wearing my usual dirty Arab garments and I pretended to be a wandering Bedouin. I saw the soldiers pointing at me and they were talking excitedly as I strolled slowly with bended back. I was hoping they would think I was a harmless old man. I waved at the train facing the soldiers as they passed me slowly and by some miracle, none of them shot at me.

I had another chance now to blow the next train and the track and with some two days to prepare. I laid the wire, but it was far too short for my safety. I was only about fifty yards away. Just as the engine rolled over the culvert, I triggered the dynamite and there was a tremendous explosion. I felt the full force of the blast which blew me several yards away and knocked me unconscious. As I came around, I staggered onto my feet and fell again. There was a horrible tear on my right leg and I began to realise that I had hurt myself quite badly. I managed to get to my feet again as I knew the soldiers would be after me. I managed to reach my men and they helped me get away and onto our waiting camels in a hail of gunshot. I never did quite discover how we survived that day and I was hit three times, two shots deflected off my binoculars and one hit the leather of my compass holder. No more wounds, fortunately but I was still in a bad way.

We managed to get back to our hideaway without further mishap although two of my men had received direct hits. Two thoughts came into my mind just then; I would have to pay for a new pair of binoculars and a compass and I would have to increase the amount I needed to pay my men to retain their services. That was my last conscious thought for at least a week. I learned later that we had damaged the engine badly and the boiler had blown up, but the train and track could be repaired. They wouldn't be inconvenienced for too long unfortunately and we would now have to travel back for new stores and reinforcements.

A full six weeks went by before we were able to return to the railway fully loaded with weapons and explosives and enough stores to keep us going for months. It had taken me most of that time to recover although my doctor told me that I needed a very long rest and recommended a return to Simla or indeed a year in Blighty. Both options were not for negotiation as I was under huge pressure from my superiors. Our army was making good progress north and hadn't lost a battle. They were confident of taking Baghdad in a couple of months although why they wanted to beats me. It wasn't a lovely place and had little strategic value although politically it was important. Bloody politics! Why does it always get in the way of proper soldiering? The only reason we were in this stinking country was to protect our oil sources, but they were hundreds of miles away down south. I knew I couldn't be away too long as I was needed to protect the army from wild Arabs and to keep it supplied by the good chaps. I also knew that we desperately needed more information about the enemy and its movements and I was the only political officer in the area. I had to be quick but effective.

We had to travel by night and managed to avoid the enemy camps and patrols. We found the line and after a couple of days of recce, I came upon the perfect place to blow up the train and cause maximum damage. The line crossed a small bridge over a dry wadi and I had a chance to destroy an engine and a couple of carriages, hopefully taking dozens of soldiers. This time, I had a larger force and carried a mortar and Lewis machine gun with two men trained to use them, both officers in our army. I attached the dynamite under the track and hid the wire in the bridge scaffolding as I climbed down. This took me a couple of hours and by the time I finished, all this equipment was well hidden from view. I buried the wire some two hundred yards leading towards a low wall of rocks where we were hiding. I had a line of my men in the rocks and ordered them to find firing positions but to keep well hidden. The mortar and machine gun were higher up at the end on the line and would be level with the end of the train when it finally arrived. I had discovered that the next train was due later that afternoon.

I was certain that I had laid the charge and the wire correctly and all we had to do was wait but not for too long. I saw the train with eight carriages rumbling along the track from about two miles away. This time, I was going to make it work. Just as the train was about to touch the bridge, I pressed the plunger. There was a vast explosion with plenty of fire and black smoke: the bridge was destroyed, and the engine crashed down into the wadi pulling three carriages with it. The other five carriages had broken free and slowly ran back down the slope away from us. This was a great success and for a moment, I felt huge relief after these months of hard work.

I knew many Turkish soldiers had been killed and this gave us a better chance of getting away unscathed but there were still hundreds in the other carriages and it didn't take them long to climb out of the carriages on the far side. The mortar and Lewis machine gun officers were to my right where the hill climbed to a level which allowed them to fire over the train and at my signal, they fired: we mowed them down and also damaged the other carriages beyond reasonable repair. Their soldiers didn't have the stomach for a fight and dozens ran away on the far side back towards a nearby town. Unfortunately, some of my newer Arab recruits only saw opportunities for plunder and to my extreme frustration, ran down to the damaged carriages. Any remaining passengers were slaughtered, and all their valuables taken along with luggage and stores. Some brought their camels to the train to load their plunder and get away. There was nothing I could do to stop them.

Whilst my loyal men watched, they wouldn't condemn their friends nor take any action. The plunder took an hour and afterwards, the raiding Arabs disappeared into the desert. I took some charges down to the track to ensure that the engine and carriages could not be repaired but I was aware I had to be quick. Enemy forces would have been alerted and their reprisals would be deadly.

As we fled on our camels, I felt elated that we had been successful at last, but it had taken its toll: I had lost many men killed and wounded and had used up much of my resources of animals, equipment and money. In addition, I had suffered wounds and illness and I had had to push myself hard to achieve results. I had lost more weight and guessed I had shortened my life somewhat. We hurried back to our army down south and I took the opportunity to visit an army doctor again, but I had guessed what the bloody quack would say. He suggested that I go back to India for a few months, but our army was heading towards Ctesiphon on their way to Baghdad and they urgently needed my help.

I made contact with Eddie: "Gerald, we urgently need to know what we are up against. So far, we have won every battle, some with difficulty, but our enemy has been poorly trained, and their supporting Arabs were not good fighters. I know from you that crack troops from the Dardanelles are joining them. I need to know how many with as much information as possible about them. You have got two weeks before we engage the enemy and we must know beforehand."

I took my small group of a dozen loyal Arab fighters up north: we had been together for over a year now and had fought in dozens of engagements. We managed to slip behind enemy lines without incident and we headed for a small village near to Baghdad. There I knew we would get the information we needed, and it would be accurate. Two weeks later, I was able to report back to Eddie with numbers of men, names of the regiments involved and the guns involved.

"That's damn bad news but many thanks for this information. We will be outnumbered, and these are all crack troops. I have had different information from Basra which suggested that numbers are far fewer. Despite the use of our aircraft, I am getting poor intelligence from all other sources. Meanwhile, we are short of food for our men and could use some sheep, wheat and fruit. Anything you can get us. We actually need medicines, doctors and nurses but you are not a miracle man!"

"That's a pity because I thought I was!"

Eddie gave me more gold coins as we both knew this was the best way to bribe and pay the local Arabs.

And so, I was constantly on the move all over the country and had been going non-stop for many years in this way. I had worked all over Arabia and above in Turkey, Macedonia and Greece and even as far as Russia. There was no time to rest now.

Kut al-Amara:
Eddie's Trapped Army

Their lives cannot repay us—their death could not undo—
The shame that they have laid upon our race.
But the slothfulness that wasted and the arrogance that slew,
Shall we leave it unabated in its place?

Rudyard Kipling

I was at Kut when we surrendered to the Turks. It was a shameful day for our British Indian Army. We had made such good advances over many months with relatively few casualties while fighting our way up the Tigris—we nearly got to Baghdad. We were only about twenty miles away at Ctesiphon—we used to call it Pistupon—where that huge arch is—my God, it's impressive—and just as we thought, we had won an important victory, thousands more of the enemy came up in support—we found out later that Basra had received this intelligence and these fresh troops were coming to join their fellows at Pistupon but they had omitted to tell us. But Gerald Lightman, our Political Agent, was right as always and fortunately, I had believed his reports over the official ones. But unfortunately, my superiors did not believe either him or me. To make matters worse, Gerald told us that these were crack troops brought down after their successful campaign in the Dardanelles. As usual in this campaign, we had poor supplies and no effective back up and just not enough manpower to defeat them. I was so proud of my men who had fought with the most incredible bravery even when they were exhausted—they kept on advancing and fighting, but our casualties were awful. I would say that the real outcome was a draw—in our favour but we still had to withdraw. Oh, all right, we were in full retreat.

We had been in Mesopotamia for about a year fighting our way up the Tigris and we had been very successful and hadn't lost a battle yet. When we first arrived in Mespot—one of our chaps couldn't pronounce the full name and the nickname stuck—our army had already fought and taken the southern part of the country, attacking and securing the important port of Basra. Someone said Basra was fifty miles up the arsehole of Mespot and they weren't wrong. Flooding often prevented armies from crossing this flat country and we had to travel by boat or march alongside the rivers Tigris and Euphrates where we could. Most of the irrigation systems had broken down due to lack of maintenance. The rivers were very difficult to navigate in places and often became too shallow to allow all our ships through, although the rivers swelled during the rainy season. Travelling by ship was, of course, far preferable to the slog of marching. Much of the place was infested by mosquitoes and a complete lack of sanitation caused diseases such as smallpox, plague, malaria, cholera, typhus and dysentery. And of course, most of the time, it was incredibly hot and steamy and occasionally, extremely cold and very wet. One day, we had huge chunks of ice falling on us and we had to take cover to avoid serious cuts and injuries.

Most of my fellow officers and I believed that we had advanced too far north too early and therefore, the supply and support for our army was too slow and infrequent and at times, non-existent. There was a lack of medical equipment, drugs, nurses and doctors and very poor facilities for the wounded and diseased. We were also only too aware that we had invaded Mespot as a foreign force and were imperialistic invaders who had no right or reason to be here. We had too few friends in this country and had made few efforts to foster allies. Consequently, the enemy were supported by most of the local population and fought with them against us and in fact, I believe that this was the deciding factor at Pistupon: mounted Arabs charged our flank and finally forced us to withdraw. However, we never had enough men to be successful.

We couldn't understand why our superiors were so determined to continue to try to capture Baghdad which had no strategic importance. Baghdad had lost its mythical status years ago and was just another shabby city of no real use to us. The fabled days of caliphs and magic lamps were long gone. Our seniors in London and India were determined to seize it perhaps just for propaganda reasons (rather like their determination to capture Jerusalem in Palestine). They also wanted to seek revenge for our terrible defeat in the Dardanelles at Gallipoli. There our armies had fought the Ottomans on three fronts and they held out against us. Our men were fighting over a strip of land only twenty miles by five with a third of a million men including our brave ANZAC forces and were forced to retreat with terrible losses without getting anyway near to Constantinople (or Istanbul as I should have called the city). We weren't there, of course, as we had been busy slogging our way north in this horrible country.

Here our main mission was to protect our oil interests in the south near Basra just across the Shatt-al-Arab River in Abadan, Persia where we had the refinery and the one-hundred-mile pipeline to its source, the oilfield at Ahwag. Johnny Turk was determined to capture the oil wells and refinery for himself and then immobilise our shipping and army which we could not operate for a week without oil. However, if we had dug in around Basra up to say Qurna a few miles up the river, we could have controlled and protected the whole region. Qurna incidentally was the site of the legendary Garden of Eden—well, if you have seen the town and area, you would find this hard to believe. I suppose the Garden might have been beautiful once upon a time but there have been so many wars in this region over the centuries that most of the land had become polluted and water systems had been abandoned. Qurna at least had swaying palm trees and numerous date palms with very colourful flowers, reminding us that we were in the ancient land of the Bible. Qurna was the site of our first battle adventure and we captured the place with relative ease. We just sailed our armada up the river and made them believe that our force was much bigger than it was. This was a great victory and our easiest to date. I can't remember any of our men being injured or killed.

Back to the oil; did I mention that we British had a fifty-one per cent interest in the Anglo Persian Oil Company which owned the site? Winston Churchill had cleverly bought a controlling interest for two million pounds. British prospectors had discovered the oil some seven years before. Before oil, we operated our shipping with coal—and in many cases, still did. Can you imagine the extra labour we needed to load the coal into the huge furnaces of these ships—sometimes one hundred men were needed: not to mention the loading work and the time all this took?

We had none of those difficulties with oil and we were converting our ships at a fast rate. An additional and valuable advantage was that our warships could increase their speed from twenty knots to twenty-five and it was obvious to me and the rest of us that the countries owning the oil had superiority over those which did not. Also, more and more of our land transport was petrol powered rather than by animals. Our Abadan refinery was yielding ten thousand barrels a day and this more than doubled towards the end of the war. Hence, our determination to protect our interests. Of course, the Ottomans could see the advantage as well as we could, and they were just as determined to seize it for themselves.

Mespot had other advantages as well. The vast flat irrigated land was a potential breadbasket: with proximity to our own India and the ever-present threat of famine this could be invaluable for us. But my God, it needed a lot of work to get the waters into working order and the land back to how it used to be. It was now a disease-ridden swamp: so, we had several good reasons for being here, but we should have involved the local people more and worked for their benefit as well as ours in unison. This might have made our life much easier and given us superiority over our Ottoman enemies.

Back to the battle: a couple of memories of Pistupon will stick with me: I had a long jump champion in my command who, when we couldn't break through the barbed wire, took a running jump and soared over the top. We roared and cheered him as he charged the enemy and of course he was quickly cut down. His bravery inspired the men who then ran up to the wire under heavy fire, laid down wooden planks and charged over the top, eventually capturing the first line of enemy trenches: the second involved our general, of whom more later, who stripped off his uniform right in the middle of the battle and ordered his servant to run to get him a replacement uniform over one mile away!

I mentioned before the valuable intelligence Gerald had managed to get to us, but my seniors did not believe him and preferred to rely on information from Basra and the Flying Corps which was invariably wrong. Gerald often managed to slip through the enemy lines almost as far as Baghdad. He disguised himself as an Arab and looked and smelt the part and spoke the lingo. He also managed to trade with some of the locals to provide our moving army with essential meat and corn. He bought fields of sheep for us and kept us sustained when our people in Basra failed to do so.

We lost so many men at Pistupon with almost one in three killed or wounded. They had more men in reserve, but Gerald had predicted exactly what would happen and I had absolute trust in him and not with our own official sources. Pistupon was our first setback since we arrived here a year ago. We fought well but to a standstill and stalemate—and as I mentioned, we had no proper back up from Basra—we had to retreat down the Tigris— God, that was a terrible march: there was incessant rain and we were bogged down in mud and of course we had to carry our wounded with us. To make matters worse, our supply barges were stuck on mud banks: and the enemy were after us. We dared not be left behind knowing that those who fell would likely be captured and tortured by Arabs. We covered something like forty miles in thirty-six hours. I felt so sorry for our sick and wounded but fortunately, we were eventually able to get them on to our boats to take them on the last part of the journey. We were exhausted when we got back to Kut and we dug in there. Fortunately, our men we had left there had food, water and shelter ready for us. What a relief that was.

Whilst my men had suffered their worst casualties at the battle, I had been quite lucky so far. Yes, I had suffered jelly belly a few times from drinking the river water and was quite seriously ill. It took me several weeks to recover each time and, unlike our general who was sent back to India to have the same condition treated, my men and I had to recover on the move. Well, they did transfer me to a river steamer so at least it was quite restful. I had also suffered a small leg wound back at al Amara but this had largely healed. Afterwards, I walked with a slight limp and had to use a stick in later life. Apart from the usual mosquito bites and heat stroke which everyone suffered from, I had escaped relatively unscathed, but I had lost too many good men either killed or wounded.

Kut was a small scruffy town occupying part of a sharp loop of the Tigris, roughly two miles long and a mile wide and the river was fast flowing and around four hundred yards wide. Kut had around six thousand inhabitants and there were twice that number of us including support staff. There were several hundred mud and brick houses in the town and the whole place was smelly and unhygienic with open sewers on the streets. We used to take great care when walking through the town. On the way north, we had captured the town without great difficulty and we had large reserves of food and military stores there and now we had returned.

The Arab Muslim residents of Kut were mostly happy to stay here with us. Arabs from outside the town who supported the Turks would have slaughtered them given the chance. Some residents did, however, try to escape across the river and most were shot before they got there. We did, however, discover some spies within the population and we shot half a dozen of them.

Our general had decided that we would settle in at Kut and defend it. Our men, he said, were too tired to carry on. Yes, we needed to rest up for a day and then we could have escaped south and several of his senior officers told him so. We did, however, find the energy to dig six miles of trenches to defend ourselves. He said that he also had the interest of the residents at heart and this was a moral obligation. I did not believe him as I knew he had a low regard for anyone not British. He even despised the Indians in our force though they made up the larger proportion of our army. I reminded him that he had constantly lectured us that 'movement is the law of strategy' and that we should escape now while we had a chance, but he dismissed my comments.

He also claimed that by holding Kut, we could prevent the Turkish Army travelling south but this was clearly a falsehood as the enemy later bypassed us to block out relieving forces. At least he had disagreed and fought with his superiors both here and in London about the need to advance to Baghdad. We were over-stretched and in this, he was right. Within three days, the Turks had sealed off the entrance to the loop and our escape option had gone.

After much lobbying from us, our general finally allowed the cavalry to escape and they were led by my good friend, Gerald Lightman, who amazingly had managed to smuggle himself into

Kut through enemy lines and had then managed to escape out. He led them over our bridge across the river and took them safely across the difficult terrain through to our forces further down the river. He was incredibly brave to have smuggled himself into Kut spiriting himself past many thousands of enemy forces. He deserved to be awarded the highest honour for his actions, but this never happened. Knowing Gerald as I did, he wouldn't have given this a moment's thought. This was one of his very many courageous deeds he performed over the many years he served his country. With him gone, this left us without an experienced political officer to deal with the local population and speak their language. Some of us thought that we should have let the local population go at the same time leaving more food and supplies for ourselves, but we could have been putting all their lives in danger.

We all felt rather jealous that the cavalry had got away and left us behind to our fate. It certainly left us with fewer mouths to feed over the coming months. Before Gerald left, we had time for a short chat to discuss our rather desperate situation. He was certain that we could all escape south if we left immediately but our general had once again dismissed the idea. He often said that our relief forces would soon break through the Turkish lines but as time went on, this became less and less likely. Gerald was certain that we had walked into a trap which we had laid for ourselves and I could only agree with him.

Our general had earlier ordered us to build the pontoon and boat bridge across the river to the mainland so that we could cross it and prevent the enemy building up forces on that side of us as well. We would have been surrounded otherwise. This seemed to make sense until the Turks used the bridge to try to cross into the loop where we were. Fierce fighting took place and with some incredible bravery displayed by our chaps, we beat them back. The general then realised that the bridge had to be destroyed. I was detailed to take some engineers and some of my Gurkhas across the river to ensure that the Turkish moorings were broken so that they could not access the bridge or use it in another place. Preferably, we should destroy the bridge.

After discussions with my team, I detailed two lieutenants, one from the Royal Engineers and one from my Ghurka Regiment, to float a large plank of wood for the men get across.

They were ordered to travel silently and carry fifty pounds of explosives to set at the Turkish end. It was an extremely cold but a clear and dry night and my brave men stripped off and slipped into the water pushing and guiding the plank alongside the bridge across almost five hundred yards of river. The water was extremely cold, but the men continued without complaint. They had to travel very quietly and slowly; any detection by the other side and the game was up. I think they were more afraid of letting our general down than being attacked by the Turks, but this was a very dangerous situation.

It seemed that hours had gone by before they pulled alongside the bridge at the Turkish end near to their moorings. I could only see vague outlines from the bank, so I had to wait for their report for the full story. Minutes after they pulled away, there was a massive explosion. The bridge was ripped away from the bank and broke into pieces and smoke and flames filled the night. Rapid fire broke out immediately from the Turkish side. Neither side could use the bridge now and the realisation that we were completely trapped in the loop suddenly hit home to me.

The operation had been a complete success but almost failed in the final minutes. My lieutenant reported back and said that one of our chaps lay on the bridge, badly wounded from the earlier conflict and as they were setting the explosives, he cried out to them. The men tried to quieten him and pulled him on to the plank to take him back, but he kept crying out. They were left with no choice but to pull his head under the water; otherwise they would all have been detected—indeed it was a miracle they weren't. The man who struck the match to light the fuse said it made a shocking noise in the deadly quiet of the night and he was amazed that the Turks never heard it. I was able to report back to our general that the operation was a complete success.

We had arrived in Kut early in December that year, this would have been 1915, and the following month, the heavens opened: we had unprecedented rainfall and the level of the river became higher than the land on our peninsula. We spent days trying to drain the excess water with constant digging and building earth barriers to the river. The work was absolutely exhausting, and we struggled to protect the town and our trenches, particularly as we were on half rations by then. That is one of my clearest memory of that bloody place and it will haunt me to my dying day, which incidentally could have taken place at Basra, but it didn't—thanks to Herbert and his men.

One of the biggest problems we suffered was boredom. Most of the time, we were cooped up in the loop with nothing to do and we had to man the fort and the trenches. The fighting took only up a relatively short time of the months we were stuck there. It was a hell of a winter and we froze in the cold and were soaked in the rain. And of course, we were hungry as our stores reduced and we had no way of bringing more food in.

There were lighter moments which happily distracted us: a plague of small green frogs hopped around everywhere having arrived in the rising river. One bright chap suggested that we could arrange frog races between our trenches and everyone enthusiastically agreed. I chose one which looked stronger and fitter than the others. It was like choosing a winning horse at Sandown and I was quite good at that. I named mine Fearless Fred and I painted a small red dot on his forehead, so he could be easily identified, and no one could steal him. I spent some time talking to him and training him to be a winner. This became extremely important to me and much money and tobacco was staked.

At the first race, he was up against twelve others and at the off I encouraged him by shouting out his name. He looked round, heard my voice, put his head down and hopped like a demented kangaroo. Unfortunately, the damned animal lost his first race— in fact, he came last. I decided that he needed much more preparation and training. I spent hours coaching and training him and making him hop uphill until I was satisfied that he was fully fit and a match for the best. Eventually, he won dozens of races earning me some precious cigarettes and a noggin or two of Scotch before surprisingly producing tiny tadpoles! Then some other chap found out the frogs were delicious roasted on an open fire and the racing abruptly stopped.

Once the frogs had disappeared, we tried very hard to find other food sources: the Tigris only gave us mud fish (horrible flavour and gritty as the name suggests), starling and sparrow pie (short on meat!) and roast partridge (my favourite and a great change from mule steaks!).

We had no easy way of escaping out of our loop as the Turks had us sealed in like a cork in a bottle. As I mentioned before, many of us like Gerald believed we should have tried to escape further down the river before they blocked us in, but our general had only allowed the cavalry to ride south when we got there. If we had escaped, then we would have been nearer our supply boats and we could have joined up with our other forces; but here we were with nowhere to go. I told the general and other superiors many times that we should have forced our way out, but my voice was ignored along with several of my colleagues, but it was probably too late now. The Turks had around thirty Krupp artillery pieces and with constant shelling quickly reduced the town to rubble. We had to dig under the buildings to create basement spaces for safety.

I was in charge of the fort and our network of trenches beyond the town. The fort was situated at the top of the loop facing the enemy and the trenches ran alongside and in parallel rows all the way to the town about a mile away on the left side of the base of the loop. To begin with, the Turks bombarded the fort which was only built with mud and bricks and they managed to severely damage it. Whilst we could return some artillery fire, we could not stop this battering. After a particularly heavy burst, we knew what was coming: their guns stopped and after a period of deadly silence, the air was rent with the noise of hundreds of the enemy charging towards us yelling at the top of their voices whilst advancing across the flat no man's land. It was a terrifying experience, but my brave and well-trained men stood firm. When the enemy were in range, we fired and fired, and rows of men were cut down like corn. The rattle of machine guns was incessant and ear drum shattering. But they kept coming and we kept firing.

They broke through in two places and cut up our men with knives and bayonets. I detailed more men to the breaches and we were able to force them back. By nightfall, there were hundreds of the enemy dead or dying, almost filling the flat land all the way to their trenches. We heard the terrible cries of the wounded and many were screaming for water. One of my men asked if we could send them some in water bottles and I agreed: we threw the bottles into their midst and some at least slaked their terrible thirsts. We also threw some bread into the mass of bodies and I was pleased to see a few hands grab the pieces. By dawn, the field was deadly quiet but then the bombardment started again.

The fort was pounded once more and some of their guns were also trained on the bazaar in the centre of the town where unfortunately our hospital was situated, and it was hit many times.

The pounding of our positions carried on and to relieve the boredom, we played a game of trying to recognise all the guns we were facing by their sounds. One of these guns was a very ancient mortar which we did not spike effectively at Pistupon which the Turks subsequently captured. We nicknamed her Flatulent Flossie for her unmistakeably gassy outbursts. Another we recognised soon became Frolicsome Fanny as she had a high-pitched squeak when she fired and yet another made a popping sound and she was named Windy Lizzy. It helped to pass the time and our humour was a blessed relief in these awful times.

And then the second charge came, much fiercer than the first and we could not stop them. They broke through in several places of our fort and trenches alongside and fierce hand-to-hand fighting ensued. Eventually, we beat them back, but our losses had been severe. And then they came for the third time in even greater numbers…

Our general, Charles Vere Ferrars Townshend—he liked the men to call him Charlie except that is the Indians whom he loathed and disrespected—was an odd fellow. His personality was an extraordinary mixture of arrogance, self-promotion, showmanship and egomania. I had never met anyone who was remotely like him.

Yes, he was a brilliant general and deserves credit for a very successful campaign so far—apart from our draw at Pistupon: we didn't lose the battle, but we didn't win it either. His strategy so far had been almost faultless, and our casualties were low, but we shouldn't have advanced to Pistupon—it was a step too far. Was this his fault? Yes, I think so as he was ultimately in charge as he was the general at the front. If he felt he needed to disagree with the orders from above, or indeed from south of us, he could, of course, have resigned rather than disobey. He was highly educated, very intelligent and came from a long line of successful military leaders. He had studied historic battle strategy more than most and applied his knowledge with outstanding effect. He had had years of battle experience in places such as Egypt, the Sudan and India and had made an excellent name for himself. If all these positives were put together without his negatives, he would have been a greater general than Napoleon himself who, incidentally, he greatly admired, often copying his mannerisms—much to our annoyance. But the negatives were his undoing. His other heroes were Hannibal and Wellington and one of his principles of war was to attack and not to be passive—quite the reverse of what he had decided here in Kut.

In past campaigns, he had been known for endearing himself to the men by socialising with them in the evenings, playing the banjo and singing dirty songs, often in French. This used to annoy the officers and they despised him for this. He was a Francophile and the men nicknamed him Alphonse which I think he was rather pleased with. He used to plaster the walls in his quarters with Art Nouveau posters. Earlier, he had married an aristocratic French lady, believing that this improved his credentials. I thought he was a rather unpleasant, frenchified self-advertiser.

I had come across him several times in the past, first in South Africa where I had made him look a fool—well, he deserved it; I was defending Herbert Messenger who was in court for trumped up charges. And then latterly, I knew him in several places in India and the North-West Frontier. He never liked me and took every opportunity to put me down and frequently gave me the most unpleasant and difficult jobs.

Townshend did not want to be here in this backwater of Mesopotamia believing that this was beneath him. He thought he should have been given a senior command on the Western Front. He had a low regard of his superiors and constantly complained to us about them.

He cared more for his wretched dog, Spot, than he did for his men. In Kut, he took him for daily walks rather than spending time visiting the sick and wounded. My good friend, Crispy, once walked in on him while he was beating Spot with a cane. The winter had become extremely cold and Spot had been lying next to Boggis, Townshend's servant, just for warmth. Townshend defended his action by saying that Spot was sleeping with Boggis and that he had to learn. Crispy expressed his disgust and was made to suffer later. By the way, Crispy was Lt Col Ernest Cripps, one of the bravest man I had ever met.

Townshend could never admit that he had made a mistake by shutting himself into Kut and blamed his men, the Indians, his superiors and even us, his officers, in fact anyone rather than taking the trouble to look in his own mirror. We had an extremely difficult time with him. When we arrived there, we told him that this place looked like a trap which would be difficult to get out of. We told him should leave before the Turks got here and try to join up with our own forces further south. He, of course, ignored all our advice as he always knew best.

I remember once going to him with the other officers for our daily briefing and he was jumping up and down with frustration, all because the general leading the relief force at that time was junior to him. He would refuse to be rescued by a man of a junior rank. We were horrified with his behaviour. Another time, Crispy was there when Townshend heard that the general had been promoted above him. He was furious and Crispy witnessed floods of tears!

Townshend ordered this daily meeting at his quarters in the town and under the dreadful circumstances, this was essential. Instead of the expected discussion sharing views of all present before decisions are made by consensus, these meetings were more like lectures. Most of us put up with his dictatorship but Crispy stood up to him every time. Crispy was a lovely fellow who became a life-long friend and I had enormous respect for him. He was on the receiving end of punishments and horrible jobs as I also occasionally was, but he never flinched. It would take much more than Townshend to frighten him, if indeed anyone or anything ever did. I think he was the most courageous man I had ever met.

In addition to his blood-thirsty battle courage, he displayed quite outstanding almost God-like heroism when the surrender finally came. Crispy was wounded and quite unwell but wouldn't give up or give way. He and the other officers were separated from the ranks and whilst they suffered the most horrible treatment, the officers were offered relatively lenient but rather boring imprisonment in several camps until the end of the war. Not Crispy though: he got out of his hospital bed and marched towards his men who were being escorted out of the camp by Turkish guards.

Over many months, he took every opportunity to shout and swear at his Turkish guards to protect and spare his men and he also complained to the Turkish government and to British officials when he had the opportunity. He had a great compassion for his men and insisted on going with them to their hell although he was forcibly separated from them, he kept returning to his men. I heard about his extraordinary bravery many months later after I had arrived in India. If I hadn't been so badly wounded, I often wondered if I would have had the guts to do the same; I hope that given the situation, I would have behaved properly but I will never know. Only one of the other officers followed him and both fully knew what to expect.

The terrible treatment of our British and Indian men by their Turkish and Arab guards was one of the worse scandals in our history; they were fed contaminated food and water and most became seriously ill. They were beaten and raped and would be left where they fell, and thousands died on that terrible journey as they were force-marched north to Baghdad and on to Turkey. When they arrived in Turkey, they were treated as slaves and made to dig tunnels for the railways. Amazingly, Crispy survived to reach the camps and worked with his men carrying and breaking rocks. Very many died of disease and exhaustion and only a third of them made it back to Blighty. No one ever stood up in court to answer for these terrible crimes.

At the surrender, Townshend was taken to Baghdad by motor boat and later lived in luxury in Turkey, eating in the best restaurants and sipping expensive wines during his captivity as an honoured guest of the Turkish government. He rarely criticised his hosts for their treatment of his men either during the war or after and in fact became close friends with several of the senior figures and no one ever had to face justice for these terrible crimes.

After the war, Crispy returned to India and his incredible story was relayed by his men to anyone who would listen. They worshipped him for standing up for them against their vicious guards as he would regularly shout and rage at them when he witnessed their injustices. The guards would often back off and the men believed they were afraid of him. Crispy spoke up for his men at every opportunity and at the end of the war, he lobbied senior government figures for justice which was never forthcoming. No one could have done more for our men. Many years later, our men suffered similarly at the hands of the Japanese.

Back to the present—in Kut—Townshend spent most of his days telegraphing his superiors in London and elsewhere begging for promotion and criticising Nixon and other senior generals saying that they were not up to the job and that he was better qualified. He kept his signallers very busy tapping out these messages to politicians for his own advancement and even to friends of his in the show business world. He believed that he should be promoted and be put in charge in Europe where the war really mattered, not in this inconsequential backwater.

One time, we learned from the signallers that he asked a superior to promote him and smuggle him out of Kut to resume his career elsewhere, leaving us to face the consequences. He was ordered to stay with his men. He never allowed one of us to send messages to our families and loved ones. Once again, we were horrified with his behaviour.

I told him once again that our best chance would be to break out and try to link up with our forces trying to rescue us and indeed he was ordered to do so by London. Many thousands of our soldiers' lives were lost in the four major attempts to break through the Turkish lines to relieve us and at times, we could hear them as they were very close to us. He was so annoyed by my impertinence that he planned his revenge on me for this and for my insulting behaviour to him in the past.

That evening, while I was changing my uniform before inspecting my men on parade, he came to my quarters and demanded I accompany him there and then to inspect my men. I had little more than my underwear on at the time, but I had no choice but to obey. I decided to stand tall and ignore my plight and I behaved as if I was fully dressed and kept my cool. When we inspected the men, there were one or two giggles which he enjoyed but in the most part, my men could see that he was trying to humiliate me. He didn't manage to do so.

Townshend sent out dozens of communiques to his troops where he unwisely blamed our situation on everyone else except himself and our men. He was openly critical about his superiors and our armies which were trying to rescue us and those in London and India. Our army had thousands of casualties during their tremendous efforts to rescue us. We were often very excited to hear our guns so close and some of us managed to see the battles from rooftops. Once again, Townshend was asked to break out to assist them, but he refused.

Twenty years before, he had commanded Chitral Fort in the North-West Frontier holding out against thousands of Pathan rebels for forty-six days until a relieving force came. He had five hundred men in his command and became a doyen of the British Press as the men's lives were subsequently saved. By extraordinary coincidence, the man trying to relieve him now was Lt General Fenton Aylmer who had saved him at Chitral Fort. One of my fellow officers was in this relieving force and he described the way Townshend relished the situation as he would now become a British hero.

After Chitral, he was asked to dine with Queen Victoria as a reward for his tenacity and courage. He was indeed a true British hero. Earlier, he had been part of the relieving force which tried too late to save Chinese Gordon at Khartoum. He envied the adulation which Gordon posthumously enjoyed. We often talked about him and believed that maybe he was trying to replicate his and Gordon's heroic actions so that once again he would be recognised by the people and his superiors and get the promotion and heroic status he believed he deserved. He desperately wanted to be the hero again and believed that he would be remembered for his courage at Kut.

Massive efforts were made to try to relieve us at Kut and many thousands of lives were lost in the attempt; in fact, more were killed and wounded than the total number of people stranded in Kut. For some reason, Townshend had previously informed the relieving forces that he only had food supplies for one month until the end of January. Perhaps he was trying to get the relieving forces to get to him as soon as possible. They attacked north towards Kut before they were fully prepared and inevitably failed to get through. Townshend was never forgiven for this by the authorities nor by the British public when they learned about the true situation much later.

At a morning briefing, Crispy suggested that before we give our relief army more inaccurate food estimates, we should carry out a full inventory and search every house. Not surprisingly, Crispy got this job and found tons of grain and other foodstuffs hidden away in the civilian areas. The guilty house owners hid away in fear of retribution from us. Townshend was now able to send out more accurate timescales and we discovered we could hold out, on half rations, at least for another two maybe three months. Townshend always said that he wasn't to know about this extra food but failed to search for it earlier until we prompted him. As it happened, we had to slaughter and eat our animals to survive. Horse and mule became an important part of our diet.

To make matters worse, the General Gorringe (I knew him in India—didn't care for this fellow—we called him Bloody Orange) was trying to break through. He disliked Townshend and the feeling was mutual. I think he would have liked to see him fail: I always find it incredible that petty quarrels and disagreements can cost so many lives unnecessarily. Why can't fully grown men stop acting like damned schoolchildren and put aside their differences for the sake of other men's lives? Unfortunately, I have seen this behaviour repeated many times before.

Back to the present at the fort: we had managed to beat off their third attempt to overrun us but unfortunately, with even greater losses. There were hundreds of men on both sides fighting with bayonets and knives and for a tough two hours, I was in the middle of the fighting, stabbing, jabbing, lunging and slashing at the enemy. At one time, a group of the bastards managed to corner me and trapped me against a wall. At least six of them were running at me with bayonets pointing at my stomach. Of course, I wasn't scared—I was bloody terrified! I thought this was my lot when at the last possible moment, two of my brilliant little Ghurka warriors had seen my plight and charged at them with their Kukris drawn. I almost felt sorry for the Turks as the Ghurkhas were not allowed to sheath their knives without drawing blood first, which they did, of course, to all my assailants. Miraculously, I wasn't injured. We must have killed and maimed hundreds of the enemy that day and of course had many casualties of our own. We were all absolutely exhausted at the end of it and I remember collapsing where I stood and sleeping for hours.

After this, we decided to try to gain the initiative; I lead a sortie from the fort and we ran towards the Turkish front line. We were twenty men in total but due to the food situation, we were not as fit as we should have been. We lined up, fixed bayonets and I gave the order to start walking but keeping level. After fifty or so yards, I yelled out the command to charge and pointing our bayonets towards the enemy, we ran forward howling like demented banshees. In a minute, we had reached the Turkish side still yelling at the top of our voices and I could see their terrified faces. No one had fired at us; they just looked at us, turned around and scrambled out of their trenches and ran back towards their side as fast as their legs would go. We were just too much for them and as I jumped into the lead trench, my men followed me and in seconds, we held their first line of trenches.

Initially, we were exhilarated at such an easy victory but within minutes, a huge mass of enemy soldiers was approaching from their lines with guns and bayonets pointing. There must have been several hundred and so, we lined in the trench facing them as they advanced forward. I shouted, "Hold your fire," until they were within twenty yards of us. Had I left it too late? Just then, I yelled the word "fire" and twenty guns blasted into their front line shredding the men and blowing them backwards. A second force charged towards us and once again, we fired and stopped them. The men withdrew leaving their dead and dying in no man's land between us. I looked at the men and I was relieved that not one had even a scratch on them and they were smiling and looking forward to the next encounter.

Nothing happened for around an hour and then I saw three machine guns being set up from their second trench in a wide semi-circle with around one hundred yards between them. They were massing forces on our left and right flank. I deemed this a good time to withdraw and we then could repeat the attack later with more men. As we climbed out of the trench, a few of the enemy started firing at us but thank God, their machine guns weren't ready yet. We ran back to our trenches but unfortunately had one man down just when we started running. He was killed instantly and the rest of us got back safely. We had given them a tremendous fright and I knew they would be warier of us in the future.

Then the Turks mounted a huge force against us which we repelled but at great cost of our good men. This was the last major assault against us although it was followed by a mass of deadly shells fired into our trenches and onto the fort which was now reduced to crumbled stone. I decided to patrol our trenches to check where repairs were needed and to try to boost the morale of our beleaguered men. I noticed in one trench a ribbon of bright paper had been hung against a front wall and then looped across to the back.

"What on earth is that for, trooper?"

"It's Christmas, sir and if you look into the other rows, the lads have done the same with any paper they could get hold of. The Rev Spooner is conducting a service in that dugout later and we are scrounging around for a box for the altar. Billy there has made a beautiful cross and we are looking for something to represent a chalice. Are you coming, sir?"

While he spoke, bullets were still buzzing around and I ducked to avoid them. I wouldn't miss this service and no damned Turk was going to rob me of the opportunity. The service was the most extraordinary and moving occasion and men were singing with joy whilst thinking of their loved ones at home.

I was immediately transported to my childhood at the vicarage and I was playing hide and seek with my siblings in our wooded grounds. A call came from the back door, "lunch is ready," and we stopped playing and rushed into the house. The house was full of the smell of roast beef and delicious roast potatoes. After standing for what seemed to be an interminable time for father to say grace, we sat down with our orange drinks and slavered over the forthcoming treats. Once grace was over, he ran the knife over the steel in a ceremony of carving (I never believed it sharpened the knife until I ran my finger over the blade much later). My mother added roasted parsnips (delicious), boiled cabbage (smelled like drains), crispy brown potatoes (gosh!), roasted carrots (oh so sweet!) and lashings of thick and delicious brown gravy.

I came back to the present in that instant and realised that I was drooling which could have been quite embarrassing! Of course, my thoughts and focus were with Molly and she was standing next to me. I could only see her out of the corner of my eye, but I could smell her distinctive perfume which I couldn't name but I vowed to find out after the war and smother her in it. I turned to her at my side and she was gone.

The Rev Spooner was a most remarkable man and I looked around the dugout at the faces of my friends. Tears were flowing unashamedly as everyone was lost in their private dreams and they all said their prayers with a passion rarely seen and sung the hymns with gusto and fortitude. Even my father never managed to stir up his parishioners like this and they never even came close to the dedication and devotion of this audience. All through this, the enemy never let up and the bullets still flew over our heads relentlessly. A shell fell a few dozen yards away. There was no let up for us—even on Christmas Day.

After the service, we shared around some delicacies which we had received from home over the past many months. I so clearly remember eating tinned goose and plum duff. One officer shared his mule tongue in aspic which was surprisingly good. We even had a noggin or two of whisky, and the peaty flavour and warm burn was very comforting as it slipped down. I will never forget the sensations of these delicious treats.

A few days later, I was sweeping the enemy area with my binoculars from the fort when I chanced to view the German leaders meeting and talking in a group. There was one man that I took note of: he was a small fat man bobbing up and down wearing a ridiculous round helmet with a pointy top I think they call the Pickelhaube. He looked so funny that I laughed out loud attracting the attention of my artillery lieutenant.

"Take a look at this," I said handing him the binoculars.

"Bloody hell, that's Von der Goltz isn't it?" He had just taken charge of the army replacing the Turkish leaders.

"Do you think you could lob a shell into the middle of the group? We might even hit the fat bastard if we are lucky."

"I can give it a bloody good try," he called back.

His shell landed right on target and we laughed like hell seeing these fat, self-important Germans scrambling about in total panic and falling to the ground with their hands covering their necks, terrified for their lives. It was an excellent comedy moment and one to cherish. However, I was in trouble when Townshend heard about this.

"My God, you could have killed him! Don't you realise that he has one of the most brilliant military brains? I have huge respect for him. If I ever had to surrender to anyone, it would be to him rather than those amateur Turkish fellows. Don't try that stunt again."

You would think that he would be pleased if we had eliminated their general and thrown their army into confusion but no, it was more important that he was saved because of his military ability and reputation. If it was up to me, I would have pounded the area to ensure we had killed him. When I told my colleagues about this later, no one was at all surprised, but some thought it was time to mutiny. I believe we got very close to carrying this out on several occasions.

Meanwhile, life in Kut was getting worse by the day. We were being pounded by their guns almost all the time. It was apparent that the enemy leadership, now run by the Germans, had ordered a change in tactics: there would be no more attacks to our line but instead, we would be slowly starved into submission. The debilitating hunger was an awful long torture and my digestive system was all over the place. One morning as I was shaving, I looked down and was surprised to see my stomach had shrunk inwards and my ribs were clearly on view. At another time, I would have been pleased to lose my paunch but now, as I grew weaker, it was the last thing I needed.

Our animals were hungry as well—those we hadn't killed for food yet and one officer complained that his horse had eaten its blanket over night. I think it was more likely that the blanket was stolen by a cold Arab!

There seemed to be a depressing inevitability about our situation. This was a long downhill journey which none of us were enjoying and we were dreading the ending. We all really knew what was coming but could not think about it and dare not imagine it. For soldiers like us, it was the worst possible ending to a campaign. We didn't know what to expect if the surrender came but most of us did not fancy our chances with the Turks and their Arab allies. I remember having the greatest difficulty getting to sleep each night with the cold and extreme hunger but when I finally did, the sleep was very deep. Sometimes, I dreamt of my childhood and of course everything was warm and happy, and all endings were like good stories. Waking up to the reality was horrible.

Some of our men could not endure this torture and disabled themselves by shooting into their hands or feet. They were taken to the sickbay and hoped they would be treated leniently by the enemy. We all hoped our ordeal would be over soon and like the boyhood stories, have a happy ending with a last-minute rescue.

We knew that our army was fighting hard to rescue us but kept being forced back by the enemy. They got so close to us that I could often watch their progress from the rooftops of some of the houses in the town which were still standing. We could hear our heavy guns by placing our ears to the trench walls. We knew that the casualty rates were enormous and we frequently paid homage to the brave men who were so desperately trying to relieve us, but they kept being resisted and were constantly pushed back. They often had to stop, rest and regroup and reinforcements were joining them in greater numbers. Surely, we would be rescued soon.

I woke one morning and as usual, struggled to get moving. I picked up my tobacco pouch and saw that I only had enough for one pipe full. Damn! Tobacco was such a comforter and eased almost all of our stressful situations. It held back hunger and even cold. I filled my pipe and lit it, slowly drawing in the delicious smoky warmth of rich tobacco. I exhaled slowly thoroughly enjoying the warmth and comfort this gave me.

My batman brought me a cup of hot brown brew he called tea. It wasn't his fault, of course, and we had tried to make a reasonable drink experimenting some of with the local plants. We used various combinations of ginger with herbs but never managed to replicate the delicious tea we grew in India and unfortunately, there was nothing like it here. Nevertheless, I was extremely grateful to him as always.

Mentioning green plants, we even tried eating some of the herbs to go with our meat which were in plentiful supply, but we never found palatable greens and without vegetables meat becomes very difficult to enjoy and digest. I had never before realised how important it was to eat a balanced diet of meat and vegetables. Our parents always nagged us to eat our greens and now I understand the vital importance of doing so. One of our senior officers was continually searching the undergrowth for edible plants and unfortunately, chose some very poisonous greens and died within hours. He was Brigadier-General Houghton, a very good friend of mine and a popular chap with everyone. I had known him in India over many years and was very sorry about his demise. We arranged a full funeral and two hundred and fifty of us attended with Rev Spooner conducting a very moving service. We were much more careful about what we ate after that.

I was just sipping the evil looking brew when I heard a whining and droning noise; stepping out of my shelter, I looked up and saw a biplane lumbering towards us from the south. I knew immediately it was one of ours and I was thrilled to hear its noise and see the early morning sun glinting off its wings. Instinctively, I waved and saw many of my colleagues doing the same. I could see two large brown bags tied up below the fuselage and hoped they contained some desperately needed food. The plane was now over the flat land near to the town and when I saw the bags released, they fell to the ground tumbling over each other, releasing a wisp of white cloud. A group of us ran to collect the bags which were, as expected, full of perfect white flour which would enable us to make delicious white bread instead of the rough brown stuff. This gave us the first ray of hope we had had in weeks that we would get all the food we needed and would at last be rescued. We could eat again and celebrate with our friends who had come to save us.

Just then I saw another plane coming up behind and we cheered as it dropped its load but in moments, we realised with despair that the bags would land in the Tigris. Then another plane came and dropped more bags, fortunately on dry land. Within hours, we had beautiful white bread and felt restored. Over the next few days, there were more drops and we received medical supplies, dressings and other badly needed supplies. We also received some new millstones which we needed for bread making. We then asked for and received some Lira currency and some hugely valuable tobacco over the next few days. We also had new gramophone needles as the old ones in our mess were blunt and scratchy. We could now hear melodies from home but in truth, most of our records were well worn out. What wonderful presents!

Our hopes rose that we would one day be able to see our families as we had lost faith in ever getting out alive. In fact, many of my colleagues had been in deep despair and depression and had lost all hope. These valuable supplies helped to lift their spirits. We were reminded of the terrible ordeal we had all been going through and of the yearlong campaign which had taken a terrible toll on our minds and bodies. When and if we ever returned, no one would believe our stories but then I suppose there were many like us caught up in the terrible struggle in many parts of the world.

We all had a story to tell and many of us would never tell it. I longed to see my beloved siblings, mother and father and of course my new darling wife, Molly. The memories of all my loved ones brought a flood of tears to my eyes. My spirits and hopes soared with the thrilling noise and sights of these magnificent planes which came the following days, as well. They looked as fragile as balsa wood models and they seemed as if they would break up at any moment into fragments of matchwood, but they were the most beautiful sights for me and our beleaguered men.

Over the next few days, we had more drops, but it was apparent that we did not have enough planes for this work and not enough food was getting through. One plane inadvertently dropped its load on the Turkish side. Fortunately, the enemy's planes must have been occupied elsewhere but on the last day, a Fokker flew over and chased a couple of our planes away. One man yelled at him, "Fokking bloody fokker!" but doubt that he heard but it made us feel better afterwards! There were no more flights and drops after this and our hopes faded. The extra food allowed the siege to continue for a few extra days only. We didn't know it then, but this was the first time that aircraft had been used to deliver supplies—or at least to try to in a war situation. Before this time, planes had been used for reconnaissance and for dropping messages only.

Our food situation was becoming desperate. We were terribly hungry. I had never seen my bones sticking through my skin to this extent and my eyes became bulbous. Many of my men, particularly the Indians, were suffering much worse and this meant that they could not carry out much physical work and felt dizzy much of the time. They were dying in even greater numbers. To make matters worse, we were being plagued by huge biting flies by day and sand flies by night and always there were thick clouds of mosquitoes.

The Battles for Kut:
Gerald and the Rescue Attempts

NOW this is the Law of the Jungle—as old and as true as the
sky;
And the Wolf that shall keep it may prosper,
but the Wolf that shall break it must die.
As the creeper that girdles the tree-trunk the Law runneth
forward and back—
For the strength of the Pack is the Wolf, and the strength of the
Wolf is the Pack.

Rudyard Kipling

Luckily, it was a clear and dry night when we set out on that long
march to Dujaila. We were determined this time to relieve the
poor and desperate men at Kut and this became even more
important as time went on and different rescue attempts failed.
We had come so close so many times and each time, our armies
had suffered terrible losses. I had been working constantly to
gain support from the local Arabs but too many of them were
against us.

Every time we fought the Turks, a swarm of Arabs would
charge our flank causing terrible damage to our forces—not to
mention to our morale as well. I was given a small force and we
tried to anticipate their attacks and fight them before they
reached our forces. I had endless meetings with their shaiks and
tried to persuade them to join us rather than the enemy and I had
some success. One time, a shaik agreed to come across to us and
I even reported this good news to Aylmer. The shaik double-
crossed us, reporting our positions and resources to the Turks
within hours of our agreement—the bastard. I had been to his
camp just north of the Tigris a few miles back. I took a small

gunboat the few miles towards his camp that same evening and fired a couple of well-directed shells right into the middle of his camp where I knew he slept. If he managed to survive that—and I didn't care much one way or another—I hoped he and his men understood that there are grave consequences if you cross Lightman.

Sometimes, these actions were necessary to show our resolve. Weakness was greatly disrespected by Arabs and most of them now supported the bloody Turks. Our problem was that our situation at Kut had caused our prestige in this part of the world enormous damage and they believed that we were going to lose. They saw massive opportunities for looting and killing as they were convinced Kut would end badly for us and the Turks would now dominate the country. I also spent many days leading our armies across difficult terrain as I knew this land better than my own face.

Another initiative was being planned to relieve the Kut garrison and I was summoned to visit Aylmer at Hanna without delay. I should have explained that he was the commander of the forces here and was responsible to Lt General Lake now far away in Basra. I had enormous respect for this man—Lt General Sir Fenton Aylmer—to give him his full title and he had the letters VC after his name. He had earned this for incredible bravery and resourcefulness as a major in 1895 when, by an extraordinary coincidence, he finally relieved Townshend at Chitral Fort in Northern India. And now he was trying to relieve him at Kut! Aylmer was one of the bravest commanders I had ever worked with and I had plenty of time for him.

"Gerry!" Why did he always use that awful name?

"I want you to lead the chaps towards the Dujaila Redoubt and the Es Sinn defences. You know your way around this wretched country better than any man alive. This is the route I want you to take," he said pointing at the map with his stick.

I should, at this point, apologise for using this military term, Redoubt. This was simply a fort made from earth with deep trenches and long sloping sides making it difficult to attack. The Turks were experts at this kind of work having perfected their skills at Gallipoli with such devastating results. I knew this place and had inspected the fortress a few weeks ago—my God, it was invincible—but my heart sank when Aylmer showed me the route he wished to take. This was the long way around and I was unfamiliar with it. I knew the route along the path of the Tigris better than most but didn't know what to expect in this direction across unknown country, although I fully understood why, because he wanted to surprise the enemy. I guessed the route was around fifteen miles long and it would be difficult to lead the men at night. Just because I had led the men countless times before with remarkable success, Aylmer and the others always assumed I knew every part of this place which wasn't quite the case. I often took advice from the locals and I hoped I could do so again but this time, I doubted it.

I am not bragging when I say that I had achieved almost mythical status up to now and I was desperate to keep my reputation intact. They just assumed that I knew everything about this country and its peoples, but the truth was that there were many things I did not know. There were many times where my competence or lack of it was close to being exposed but usually, I managed to blag my way through situations. Suppose I messed up this time, took the men on the wrong path and missed the Redoubt altogether. We would have failed to relieve Kut once again and it would be all down to me. Even worse, if Townshend's men had broken out of Kut and were left exposed to half the Turkish Army because we rescuers were in the wrong place—well, it was just unthinkable. My reputation would be blown to bits as if it had received a direct hit from an artillery shell. No one on earth knew my secret and I intended to keep it that way.

The Redoubt was a couple of miles south of the Tigris loop which Kut was located in. Between the Tigris and the Redoubt were a couple of miles of Turkish trenches known as the Es Sinn position. If we could capture this Redoubt, we could wind up their defences towards the Tigris. This was a vitally important move.

Aylmer continued, "Townshend knows my plan and I have asked him to prepare his army in Kut to cross the Tigris and help us to rout the enemy. This will deal a massive blow to the Turks and they will have nowhere to escape to. They could turn left and cross the Shatt al Hai but the bridge is very narrow and then they will have to cross the Tigris to get back to their base. Townshend has around seven thousand soldiers and forty guns. He only has to cross two hundred yards of the Tigris and will be three miles from us by then and with our joint effort Johnny won't have a prayer. We'll have them by their danglies! But first, we have to get hold of the Redoubt and that's why we need absolute surprise."

"Who will be leading the men and how many will we have?"

"Twenty thousand men and they will be led by Kempton and Keen. Keen will lead a group breaking away from the main army and will attack the Redoubt from the west side whilst Kempton will take his men around to the east of the Redoubt. Our artillery will set off separately and you will also be responsible for getting them into position first."

My God, I was going to have to lead three sections of our bloody army at the same time in three different directions. These people must think I'm Jesus Christ!

"I think it will be better if I can stay with Kempton's lot, get them into position first and then Keen's men and finally, the artillery. I need to think about this for a few days."

"Nonsense, Gerry—what's the matter with you? Are you turning to jelly, Gerry—Ha! You've done this sort of thing many times before and you know the whole area. I have every confidence in you. Anyway, you won't have time to think—we leave at twenty hundred hours tonight!"

Well, the night was clear and for once, there was no rain, but the going was sticky with mud. The ground was flat which was a relief as I worried that there might be hills and wadis in this area. I was petrified that we would bump into enemy patrols and lose the element of surprise. I decided to travel on horseback as I had to move between positions quickly and it would be hopeless to do this on foot. I set the artillery wagons off in the direction of the Redoubt but knew I would have to keep a watch on their progress and direction as I led Kempton's group forward. All I had was a compass for direction and I detailed two chaps to measure our progress. One had a bicycle wheel and another a pedometer. No one could accuse Lightman of not utilising the very latest technology!

Most of the journey was long and dull and as I rode through the night, I had a chance to reflect on my life so far. It seems that I had been on the go for ever since I left military college for South Africa for that dreadful Boer War. I was bloodied and toughened there and turned into a ruthless killing machine. Long marches and deprivation of sleep and all discomforts had prepared me for the life ahead. It seemed that I had hardly had a break over the past fifteen years or so, but I had been back to my family in England on four occasions. I have two dear sisters who always support me and in addition to emotional encouragement, they frequently sent me warm socks and undergarments which were so valuable and indeed essential comforts for the life I was leading.

During a dozen years, I had travelled all over these lands to more than eight different countries although that could be disputed with all the changing borders mostly on reluctant camels.

I was sent to India three times and ventured north and became involved in our skirmishes in Afghanistan and the North-West frontier campaigns but mainly, I spent my time rather boringly in our offices in Simla. There were three centres of our army intelligence, the main one unsurprisingly in London, supported by Cairo and here in Simla. I was given hundreds of box files to open, examine and inwardly digest until I knew more about Arabia than most people alive. When I had time, I would trek to the beautiful Srinagar, the capital of Kashmir and into the valley and on to Mazor. This had to be my favourite part of the world with its wild forests of cherry blossom and mulberry trees, lakes and rivers:

I travelled to the Indus and Shyok rivers and then climbed up thousands of feet towards Nepal and Tibet. This had an incredible effect on my view on the world in more ways than one and I needed this essential therapy to counteract the effects of my harsh and brutal existence. I was able to examine my life in peace and isolation and look deep into my being to find out who I really was and understand my true purpose.

My health had been suffering in the harsh disease-ridden climate of Arabia. I knew that there were several conditions I was suffering, and I never seemed to have time to attend to these. Instead of finding time to seek out a rare doctor, the urgency of the mission always took precedence. I knew mine would be a short life and I wondered if the bugs or bullets would get me first. I had survived so many seriously dangerous episodes that perhaps I had become blasé and perhaps believed that my life had no value and little purpose. I resolved to take better care of my mental and physical health in future.

When I came back, I fell in love for the first time in my life. She was the niece of the Lt Governor and she stayed with him and his wife while her family were in America and she planned to live here for a couple of years. I had, of course, had several relationships with women before, but this was totally different. I was completely smitten and the idea of ever leaving the side of Julia again was beyond my imagination. I had no inclination to go travelling again and I dreaded having to return to my life in Mespot. We had a frantic social life and many days riding and boating or going for long walks in the hills. Finally, our time together came to an end. Shakespeare described parting as such sweet sorrow, but he could not have known my despair. After two of the happiest months of my life, we were parted, and I returned to the hell of Arabia.

****

The artillery had left an hour earlier, and the gun wagons were hauled by horses with ammo wagons pulled by mules also carrying packs. I decided it was time to review their progress and I spurred my horse forward and caught up with them after a short while. I could hear them before I could see them, and they were making no effort to keep the noise down. They could be heard from miles away. I rode up to the brigadier leading them.

"Can't you keep the noise down? We'll have every bloody Johnny after us bringing the whole army with them at this rate. And by the way, you are several degrees off course. You need to move in that direction."

One of my problems was that I was given the responsibility for this venture without the rank. The brigadier was senior to me—to put it mildly—but I hoped he would take my advice and understand the necessity of surprise. Unfortunately, we did not like each other—this may have had something to do with my comments to him at the battle of Wadi when he got hopelessly lost and his incompetence probably contributed for our loss of the battle and the death and wounding of many good men. My choice of words was probably not wise then and I had toned them down considerably on this occasion.

"Why don't you piss off and chase one of your favourite goats, Lightman. I won't take orders from you and I don't rate your so-called expertise in this matter. I don't think you've got a fucking clue where we are going anyway. There are no enemy forces around and not a chance we will be heard." He must have been a member of the 'Lightman for president club'!

Just then a pack mule managed to break away from the column and raced on ahead and his mate followed him. Their loads were thrown crashing to the ground but worse, the mules made a horrible high-pitched braying and bellowing cacophony which would have woken up every Turk from Eden to Babylon.

"Brigadier, you've got a strange way of trying to achieve surprise. You can be sure that when this venture goes tits up— which it will if you carry on like this—you will be held fully accountable by me."

I heard a small cheer from a couple of his men who clearly agreed with me and I sped away back to the main column before he could make his usual acid reply. I caught up with Kempton— that's Brigadier-General Kempton—and told him about the artillery's situation. I suggested that we overtake them and led the way to the Redoubt. Fortunately, he agreed with me and we went forward. I suggested to him that we now form a column of men four abreast which he also agreed to. This would be much more practical if we bumped into Johnny.

Later, my next problem occurred: the men in the front fell into trench a good six feet deep and I had to find a way around it for the rest of the column. Fortunately, the trench was a natural formation and was not full of trigger-happy johnnies.

"You could have warned us about the trench, Lightman. I thought you knew the area backwards."

My invincibility was slipping! We managed to overtake the artillery in around three hours and were well on our way to the Redoubt or, so I thought. I suggested to Kempton that it was time for Keen's column to break away so that they could make their way to the east side where they would wait for the attack signal. I rode over to direct Keen's force and warned him to keep all noise to the absolute minimum and not to get too close to the Redoubt. His men would have to be out of sight when the light came and would need to dig in three thousand yards from the Redoubt. I was only repeating the instructions we had all heard earlier and he agreed with me. I rode back to Kempton. I estimated that he was only around four miles off the Redoubt.

It was such a relief to be so close now and my responsibilities were almost over, and another mission safely completed. We marched on and I thought that the Redoubt would soon be in view in the dim morning light, but still, we saw nothing. I consulted my men and they both confirmed that we should have been there by now.

"Where the bloody hell is it then?" I kept asking.

"I think we must have ventured too far south. I think we need to turn to the right travelling north to get there," my two guides advised me. God, I didn't have a clue where the hell we were and so I went along with their idea. I went to Kempton and told him we were changing direction.

"What about the bloody artillery? We need to tell them."

I rode back as fast as I could and relayed the new instructions to the despicable brigadier. I have forgotten his name since but if I could remember, I would have no hesitation in repeating it here and spoiling his precious reputation. I told him about the change of plan.

"What's the matter, Lightman, you don't know where the fuck we are, do you? Have you been at the bottle again? Bloody drunkard—no use to man or beast."

He was referring to an occasion a few weeks ago at Amara, I had consumed too much champagne at a mess dinner and had gone for a swim in the Tigris fully clothed for a bet. To earn my reward, I had to swim across the Tigris and back again. I damned nearly drowned but I made it (all right, I turned around when I was halfway across, but they didn't see me in the dark) and then needed a couple of rums to revive my tired body. I know my behaviour amused my colleagues enormously; they told me about it the next day, but I can't remember a bloody thing about it. He made it sound like I was a regular drunk—which I wasn't—and he had probably spread the gossip.

I went on the attack, "Every time I screwed your mother, she loved it so much she poured me a dram!"

You should have seen his face. He went pale with rage and then even paler until he was as white as a sheet and I thought he was going to pass out. Perhaps I had unknowingly stumbled across some home truths. I turned away and went back to my

119

troop knowing that I had made an enemy who could cause me serious problems in the future.

After another hour, I could see the Redoubt in the distance and I reported this to Kempton and later, Keen. The relief on all our faces was evident.

"Lightman—it seems very quiet there—where are the enemy? I want you to go over and find out exactly what is going on."

Bloody hell—why is it always me? I mumbled to myself and I walked with heavy steps towards the fortress. It would be just my luck to walk into the middle of several thousand Turks. Due to the huge sandbank I had to climb to see over to the other side, I would be fully exposed. They would kill me in seconds or grab me and subject me to the filthiest kinds of torture until I gave up and told them that twenty thousand men and forty guns were a few yards away and they were going be blasted to bits and then sent back to their God. As I trudged forwards, I reflected on all the hundreds of deadly situations I had survived over the years. Was I risking providence by walking into another deadly trap? Why couldn't one of the others have gone in my place—no—it was always me and it was my own fault? I had unknowingly put myself upon a high pillar above all others. Everyone assumed I knew all the locals, all the land and the river and had all the best strategies for every situation—which, of course, no man did.

"Don't worry, chaps—Lightman is here—and he will get us out of any tight spot."

"Lightman, where are the enemy and when is their artillery going to blast off? Are there more of the enemy coming in support? What are our generals going to do? Are the local Arabs honest and what's for bloody tea?"

Well, I made the last one up, but you get the picture. I reached the bottom of the slope and gingerly made my way up. Well, you had to hand it to Johnny—he knew how to make a fortress. He really had learnt his lesson well at Gallipoli. This must have taken thousands of men to build at their instructions. I bet they used the local Arab tribe—you know the one that swore undying loyalty and devotion to me and the British Army. A small matter of a larger payment had secured their services. I knew, of course, how it worked and I am sure I would be proved right. I climbed up the last few feet of the sand wall and slowly peeped over. It was silent as the grave and after waiting a couple of minutes I climbed to the top and waited. I stopped and listened again—nothing! I slid on my arse to the bottom of the slope and to the first trench and stood there very still for a couple of seconds. Nothing. Where the bloody hell were they?

I walked around the first trench and when I got to the far side, I smelled pungent smoke. I tensed knowing that a Johnny was smoking one of their foul cigarettes a few yards from where I was. So, the Redoubt was occupied after all, but it looked like the main army had left and had left a guard or two or maybe three. I knew I had to get rid of them before they raised the alarm. I spotted his supine figure in the gloom. He was resting with his back against the sloping side of the trench. I drew my knife in my right hand and crept towards him. As I came alongside, I clamped my left hand over his mouth and at the same time, plunged my knife into his side and pushed upwards. His body jerked and shivered, and I kept my left hand in place until his body relaxed, and I knew he was dead. Not a sound—I had had plenty of practice at this before. I did find one more man and did the same to him. I left their bodies where they fell.

I couldn't believe it. The whole damn place was empty! Why the hell did Johnny leave it empty? This was a good fortress and they should have kept a full battalion here at all times and it would be the devil's own job to shift them out of here. I stepped into the inner trenches just to make sure they were all clear and stood on the highest point to look towards the defences on the line of Es Sinn trenches which carried on towards the river Tigris and to Kut beyond but couldn't see any activity there either.

I knew these trenches had to be occupied but the men must have been sleeping. I needed to be careful as they would have many guards along the line. Well, this discovery was momentous. All we needed to do was occupy the Redoubt and attack out towards Es Sinn. The way would be clear to Kut and our poor men there would be free at last. We would signal Townshend to break out and boat across the river and between our two armies, we could wrap up the dreaded bastards for good. I was dizzy with excitement at the possibilities and after so long, we would have the winning hand in this horrible war.

I knew it was vital for me to get back to my army and contact Kempton. Extreme speed and positive decision making was essential for a successful outcome. Just as the light was beginning to improve, I sped over the fortifications as fast as my legs would carry me: I was breathing heavily with the extreme exercise, partly due to my lack of fitness and due to the excitement and urgency of the situation. I cursed my weakness in not keeping up my exercise routine. I had been much fitter before when tough ventures stretched my limbs and my stamina improved. Well, all right, I had been enjoying myself a bit too much in the officer's mess recently and partying for many nights in the nightclubs of Basra where I was involved in essential intelligence work.

I climbed to the top of the outer wall and fell over the top tumbling down the other side arse over end—quite undignified but I didn't care as no one was watching. Getting to my feet, I scrambled forward as fast as I could go. I still had a couple of thousand yards to cover and raced at top speed back to my army. I have tried to recall those moments but they are lost in a fog and I think my mind must have since blocked out the pain. The camp came into view at last and I desperately called out for Kempton.

"Slow down, Lightman! What the hell has gotten into your pants?"

"I must speak to Kempton now. Now, this instant—for God's sake get him! Get him now! The survival of Kut depends on him!" I shouted with my voice rising in near panic. It was essential these idiots reacted quickly. The men around me looked alarmed and a couple ran off to find someone senior. Unfortunately, they found another brigadier—I don't seem to get on with them very well—I knew him vaguely but again can't recall his name.

"What is it, Lightman? What the hell can be this important? You seem to be in a royal fizz."

"The Redoubt is empty. There are no Turks there. If we can occupy it immediately, we can wrap up this campaign and save our boys at Kut. You must act now and tell Kempton."

"Now, now calm down, man. There is no way we are going to attack now. Our orders are to wait for the artillery to get here."

"What do you mean? That fucking idiot is not here yet? What the bloody fuck is he doing? I gave him very clear directions and he fucked up. I don't believe it. Jesus Christ, the incompetence around here is just shit! Get Kempton now!"

"If you don't calm down, man, I will have you restrained."

"By all that's holy, get your fucking arses over there and hold the bloody fort. Even you cretins will be able to do this."

I wasn't doing myself any favours with my language, but I had no choice. The brigadier nodded at two of his men and they grasped an arm each very tightly. I screamed, implored and begged him but it was no use. He turned his back and went off far too slowly, presumably to tell Kempton that I had lost it completely and that I would have to be put on a charge. I slumped down and pretended to give up my mission. The men eased their grip a bit and I wrestled them free and in the same moment, sprinted off towards where I thought Kempton would be. The two men were running after me panting and cursing. They were very close, and I knew this was the most important moment of my life so far. Then I saw him. He was sitting at a table in front of his tent talking to two officers.

"Kempton, Kempton, for God's sake—you must occupy the Redoubt—its empty!" I screamed hoarsely at him. Just then the two men caught up with me tackling me to the ground, knocking out the remaining air in my lungs. I struggled to get more words out.

"This is the most important moment in this war…"

He strolled over to me calmly, slowly taking his pipe out of his mouth and said in his most condescending voice.

"Now, Lightman, you really should calm down. We are not ready to advance yet—you know our orders as well as anyone. The artillery has to be in position first and we attack at 1100 hours and not before. To go in now will cause chaos. Lightman, you are now on a charge and will be held until we get back to the Wadi. No doubt Aylmer will want to have some strong words with you. I think you need a break. We all need to rest sometime, and you have been going harder than most and overdoing it a bit lately." I slumped down once again and my tears flowed.

****

"Why the hell did you take them the wrong way, Gerry? I thought you knew the land intimately. And why didn't you tell Kempton that the Redoubt was unoccupied. My God, what a bloody cock up. Heads will roll for this and mine will be one of them."

Aylmer was furious with good reason and he was desperate to discover who was to blame for this. I was sitting in his office reflecting on the terrible losses of our men at the Dujaila Redoubt. The problem was that everyone followed his orders—to the letter—and if only some of them had used their own initiative, we wouldn't be here now. Yes, the artillery did open up at 1100 and Kempton sent in our men an hour later. By then, of course, the Redoubt was full of at least three thousand Turks. The slaughter was terrible as they were able to mow down our men in their hundreds. By sheer guts and determination, we were able to take and hold the first two lines of their trenches, but we were forced out later. This was another bloody cock up to add to the long list of our campaign to rescue our men at Kut.

In the end, we had lost around four thousand men killed and wounded at the Redoubt and eventually, we were forced to retire. We made the long march back to the Wadi from where we had started out a day or so before. I was pleased Kempton trusted me enough to ride my horse back, but I was unsurprisingly given no duties. Aylmer was shocked by our defeat and his face was red in fury and frustration. I think he knew it was the end of his command in Mespot. A procession of officers had been called in while he tried to discover who was at fault here. I knew that Kempton and that ugly brigadier had tried to put the blame largely on me. It was my fault that the artillery had not arrived as 'Lightman had given them the wrong directions' etc., etc.

There was no getting away from the fact that I had found the Redoubt empty and had urged Kempton and others to occupy it. But no, they hid behind their orders and said they could not disobey them. Bloody British Army—no bloody initiative—'I was only obeying orders, sir!' This pathetic response had largely contributed to greater losses of men than the total population of Kut. Surely, this was the biggest embarrassment to our nation since Khartoum or Isandlwana. The repercussions would be terrible, and I was determined that I would not become one of the fallen although there were plenty hoping for this outcome.

"We had miscalculated by a couple of miles and when we realised our mistake, we altered direction a few degrees to the north. I then rode off to notify the artillery. This was not the cause of our defeat despite the lies you may have been told."

"Why the hell didn't you tell them the Redoubt was empty? We could have occupied it and Johnny could never have kicked us out." He was still furious with me.

"I did, I told Kempton and many others, but they refused to go against orders. In fact, I begged him to occupy the Redoubt and he arrested me for my outburst. And if he denies this, bring him in here and let him try to lie in front of me. I wouldn't fancy his chances." I kept my cool, but inside, I was seething.

"In fact, his inaction was the total reason we lost the battle. If he had listened and acted accordingly, we would have swept up the whole Turkish Army from here to Baghdad by now. And that bloody idiot leading the artillery didn't listen to me and got lost."

Aylmer seemed to crumble in front of me as he could imagine the glory which had just slipped through his fingers. I felt sorry for him and even more so as I had greatly admired him for his courage. He looked like a broken man now and didn't deserve the inevitable disgrace. He knew I was telling the truth and I hoped he would report this accordingly. In truth, I had no doubt that he would. He still had his pride and courage and wouldn't lie to try to save his career.

Later, I was totally exonerated as I expected to be, but Aylmer lost his job to be replaced by the dreadful but effective Gorringe. I was pleased that all the others who deserved to go did so, but not by their own accord. I had my revenge but no recognition at all for what I had done. In fact, my role was completely forgotten and no gongs were thrown in my direction. That was a blessing in a way as I was able to keep a low profile, and this made my work easier. I hoped for better results now.

****

"Well, Lightman, what the hell do we do now? God knows we have thrown good men to the slaughter in the cause of freeing Kut. Our men are still dying in their thousands and the poor men in Kut are getting hungrier and weaker. And that damned Townshend isn't helping either. I can't do it all myself for Christ's sake. Why doesn't he try to break out and meet us halfway? He's just bloody stubborn and won't listen. I think he only wants glory for himself. He even asked me to let him get out of there. What? What? (This was an unfortunate turn of phrase he came out with especially when he was under pressure!). He wants to leave his men to their own fate so that he can be promoted. Confound the man! Drink old chap?"

He pushed a large glass of malt towards me. I was sitting opposite him at his desk. All the while, he was getting redder in the face and I struggled not to repeat his nickname, Bloody Orange, which he absolutely hated, but his red face was not the reason for his moniker—it simply rhymed with Gorringe.

"Now, look here, Lightman, we need ideas—new ideas to get us out of this mess. Frankly, I don't care for you or your behaviour which is often quite outrageous, now don't take offence (I didn't), but you are the only one who seems to have solutions to our problems. I must confess, you did well at Dujaila and if those idiots had used what God had given them and listened to you, we wouldn't be where we are now. If only I hadn't been wounded, there would have been a totally different outcome. Look—I need a good three weeks to get the reinforcements I need from Basra and then we will be in a position to crush Johnny (he had a pronounced lisp and it came out as cwush) and free those poor sods. Now, Lightman—what's to be done? What? What?"

"Well, the priority is to get food through to them. We have tried flying supplies in, but we didn't have enough planes. It worked to an extent though and bought us a couple of weeks at best. I suggest we think up a novel way to get food in."

"What? What?" (Oh, for goodness sake shut up!)

"I think we should try to break through by boat…"

And so, it was that I started one of the biggest and most important projects in my life so far. I had two weeks to get the rescue organised after receiving permission from the highest levels in the army and navy although they didn't hold out much hope for the venture. To begin with, I made contact with a long-term friend, Captain Charles Cowley, who knew the Tigris intimately as he had travelled north and south between Baghdad and Basra many times. He knew the moods of his tempestuous mistress with its rises and falls, sandbanks and twists and turns. He and I had had several adventures together and he had helped me reach the many tribes I needed to negotiate and trade with and to access Johnny's army so that I could sabotage and destroy his lines of communication. He had also provided me with great intelligence about the numerous tribes which inhabited the river region. Together with his long-term colleague and great friend, Bill Reed, they formed a formidable pair with years of experience. They had both worked for The Euphrates and Tigris Steamship Company for several years before this war. We shared a dark humour together which was always good for bonding. In fact, I did not really trust anyone who didn't.

"Will you both help to relieve Kut with tons of food and supplies? As you know, we have been unable to get through to them and this really is our last hope. This will give them at least three more weeks and, in that time, Gorringe assures us that his reinforcements will have arrived."

"Of course, we will do our very best."

That was settled then. I reminded them this had to be a voluntary decision as this project was incredibly dangerous. I had checked that they were both unmarried as I wasn't allowed to pressgang those who weren't. Bloody wet blankets who run the army and indeed the world now! When the hell did this criterion come into the equation? Charles and Bill contacted friends in the navy and found the ideal steamer for the task ahead: she had twin screws and could move faster than most of the river craft. This was the SS Julnar which I had travelled in before. She would be ideal for the twisting river and this required the experience and knowledge of my two chaps. Furthermore, they had to travel in the dark of the night to have a chance of getting through. They had a journey of some twenty miles to complete and had to run pass Turkish rifles and guns on both sides of the river. We all knew that this venture would be extremely dangerous but this was our last chance to relieve the men in Kut.

Charles and Bill immediately set about armour plating the sides of the ship and reinforcing the engine and steering mechanism. They stuffed hundreds of bags of flour and dried grasses to cushion the effect of bombardment. Some of the stores had been loaded at Basra and I briefed my Arab team to scour the camps and bazaars to source the tons of additional food and supplies needed. I had a team loading bags of flour, vegetables, many varieties of fruits, fields of slaughtered sheep, guns and ammunition and dozens of other essentials for our men. Of course, the prices went up with our huge demands and I had to administer the odd kicking to stop some shaiks from being too greedy. I also knew that it would be impossible to keep our intentions secret but I had to threaten some of them to prevent them running to the Turks to give away our plans—as far as they knew them—in return for some golden coins. I said that if I discovered any disloyalty, I would deliver the death sentence to the culprits and they knew well that I meant every word. Nevertheless, I knew within days that the Turks would be informed and would be ready for us but we had no other options left.

We estimated that the Julnar was now carrying over two hundred and fifty tons of stores—maybe twenty tons more and extra weight with the steel reinforcements. I asked the chaps if they could estimate the speed that the ship could now do and they concluded that without a trial run, it would be impossible to estimate. They had twenty miles to cover to Kut. They were joined in the discussion by Lt Humphrey Firman who the navy had sent to command the ship. I had no choice in this matter but was pleased with the man who gave me full confidence that he was up for the task ahead.

I was concerned about obstructions being laid in the river and arranged for aircraft reconnaissance a few days before the venture. After several sorties, they reported that there were no obvious signs of metal blockages or mines but they couldn't be sure the river was completely clear as mines could be lurking beneath the surface. We still had a fair chance of getting through to our desperate men. I was in contact with Eddie on a daily basis and I knew that Townshend was near to surrendering. Every man was praying that the Julnar would get through and bring the essential food to our desperate men.

We were fully loaded and ready to go in the afternoon but had a few nervous hours to wait for dark. We had a brief moment to say goodbye and good luck before the ship roared off slowly and then accelerating before approaching full speed. I decided to follow in my launch for a few miles although this was extremely risky. I wanted to travel with the boys on the ship but Gorringe said no very firmly. I didn't tell him I intended to follow them. I also didn't tell him that Ned Lawrence and Captain Aubrey

Herbert had asked to travel with me. They were here to negotiate the future of Kut with the Turks and I had been asked to lead them when the time came.

The bagpipes of the Black Watch gave us a memorable send off and I knew that this would not alert the enemy as they played each evening. A little later, I had arranged for the artillery to pound the Turkish positions in the hope that Johnny would get his head down and not be aware of our departure from Falahiyah. The noise from our guns was incredible and the earth rumbled causing ripples across the water. We were motoring against a steady current and I estimated we had three or four hours to cover the twenty miles to Kut before the moon was due to appear and expose us.

The first hour passed very quickly as I was concentrating hard on the stern of the ship to follow its progress. The first part of the river was fairly straight and the sharp twists and turns would come later. We were keeping lights to a minimum to keep invisible. Incredibly, it seemed that Johnny had not heard us and I prayed that that we would have a safe passage to Kut. I was amazed at the speed of the ship and knowing its massive weight, I thought that nothing the Turks threw at us could stop its steady momentum. Surely, we would get through—we had to—this was our last chance.

A couple of hours later, we were still progressing well and I reckoned we were over halfway. Could we get there after all? I could feel the excitement rising in me. A moment later, a huge flash of light turned the night into day. The Turks had fired the largest flare I had ever seen. The river, the whole land for miles around and sky were illuminated for all the world to see and then the firing started. I slowed down and watched in horror as bullets from a hundred machine guns peppered the sides of the Julnar and then the shelling started. The first shell crashed into the water raising a huge spout of foam into the air just yards from the ship and a second crashed into the steel port side causing the ship to lean dangerously over to starboard and then right itself. Almost immediately, a third shell crashed into the bridge: Firman would be there and I knew that no one could have survived the terrible explosion. But still the ship charged forward although now at a reduced speed. We must have made another mile under continual bombardment when the Julnar hit some blockage in the water and almost came to a full stop. Its stern swung round to the bank on its starboard side and I guessed that she had hit a wire which the Turks had pulled across the river. The Julnar leaned over towards the bank like some dying elephant and I knew the game was over. As I turned my launch around and headed back, tears ran freely down my cheeks for the second time.

Kut: The Dying Days: Eddie's Starving Men

They shall not return to us, the resolute, the young,
The eager and whole-hearted whom we gave:
But the men who left them thriftily to die in their own dung,
Shall they come with years and honour to the grave?

Rudyard Kipling

When Townshend heard that the next relief attempt wouldn't be happening for a month or so, he ordered our rations to be halved once again. We had to slaughter more of our mules and horses and to ration the meat to a few ounces each per day. This was incredibly hard and unpleasant for us as no one wanted to kill our faithful and favourite animals but we had to survive. Many of our Indians refused to eat the meat on religious grounds and they became desperately thin and many starved to death. We had some senior clerics who managed to persuade the Indians that they could eat the meat for survival and would not be condemned. We even had this message confirmed on the telegraph from India but still many Indians refused, and many died; some reluctantly agreed to eat horsemeat. Disease was now rife among our men and the people and up to fifteen died each day of various ailments. Most of the men could no longer work and some Indians and Arab residents were considering switching their loyalties to the enemy. This was an extremely dangerous situation.

During these long months, the Turks were still lobbing shells on the town and the snipers never let up. We had to keep our heads down in the trenches as the snipers managed to kill and wound dozens of men. I had my hair parted by a sniper's bullet one time just as I was walking out of the fort. We were also bombed by enemy planes for a period and they were targeting our hospital. We turned our guns upwards to the sky and tried to blast the planes away, but we never hit one. If a plane had crashed I knew that our men would have torn the pilot into pieces. We seemed to be under constant bombardment.

We were constantly digging to preserve our trenches and to build barriers against the rising river. Our brick kilns were kept busy most of the time and we needed them to bolster up the collapsing trenches but eventually, we had to give up on the front line of trenches. I targeted each man to make and place two hundred and fifty bricks each day which a tough challenge under the dreadful circumstances was.

I had a message from Gerald that there would be another attempt to rescue us. He would be leading the army to the Dujaila Redoubt just south of Kut only about three miles away from us. They would attack and capture the fort and then wind up the Turk's Es Sinn trenches leading to north to the Tigris and towards us at Kut on the far bank. He asked us to prepare our army so that we could cross the Tigris and when they had successfully attacked the Redoubt, he would send us a message to get into our boats. We would then trap the Turks between our two forces.

At the appointed time, we climbed onto our flat roof and looked south. There was a massive firework display and we were hopeful that their attack would be successful. Gerald's message never came though and hours later, we retired disappointed to our quarters. We had confirmation later that the attack had failed.

There was one more very brave attempt: Gerald contacted me about another ambitious attempt to get food through to us. He was charged with preparing and sending a steamer through with tons of food and supplies which would have kept us going for around three weeks or so, perhaps allowing enough time for reinforcements to have one more attempt to break through to us. The ship Julnar was one we knew well from earlier times and we hoped it had a good chance to get through. On the night it was due, a small group of us climbed onto the flat top of our tall telegraph building, which had become our regular viewing point of our army's activities and gazed into the distance towards where the ship would come from. We watched as a massive flare lit up the sky, the river and the countryside for what seemed like several minutes and then saw the flashes of Turkish guns.

The huge booming noises and lightning bolts were like the worst thunderstorm I'd ever seen with terrific explosions: darts of fire and clouds of smoke filled the sky. I felt sorry for the ship's crew who must have been suffering a terrible battering. Surely no ship could have survived this massive bombardment which must have been worse than God's retribution. Even the building I was standing on juddered and shook and at one point I thought it might crumble beneath us. I peered into the distance through my binoculars but still couldn't see the ship or the guns which were still too far away, but I feared for the worse.

Surely, we couldn't hold out any more: we knew that we had run out of options and our surrender was imminent. I had a message from Gerald confirming that the attempt had failed which did not surprise anyone. He also confirmed that a small team of negotiators working for British Intelligence had arrived and he would be leading them to the Turkish camp. They had travelled from Cairo to Basra and then the long journey along the Tigris to us. I was more confident when he said that my old friend, Ned Lawrence, was leading the team together with the well-known political agent and aristocrat, Aubrey Herbert. I knew Ned well from our adventures in Sinai and at Carchemish. He was to negotiate our desperate situation at Kut with the Turks. I had great confidence in his ability and if anyone could save us—he could. But before he got to the Turks, my personal disaster struck.

I was carrying out an inspection of our forward trenches early in the morning and was standing inside a trench talking to my havildar about food issues. A sniper's bullet hit me in the face which flicked my head backwards and I was propelled onto my backside which cushioned my fall onto the bottom of the trench. The bullet had splintered and caused half my face to be ripped off and severe damage to my left eye and nostrils. I also lost some skull which had been chipped away. Not that I remember any of that when I woke up some hours later. I had been stretchered to the makeshift hospital in the town and taken straight into the operating theatre where our few doctors patched me up as well as they could with their very limited equipment, drugs and resources. I was unconscious and seriously ill for days.

The doctors later told me that they were very worried about my condition as recovery was being hampered by severe malnutrition and bodily weakness. They managed to secure me some extra food and gave me some precious milk.

"I think we have done the best that we can do for you. We have sewn up your face and there is no permanent damage to the area, but you need treatment in a proper hospital. Fortunately, your eyesight is OK. The Turks are aiming their shells at us, so I am moving you to the Lusitania for safety," the doctor informed me. This was a double-decked barge moored further away from the shelling on the far side of the town. I vaguely remember being stretchered away.

One afternoon, I couldn't sleep and there seemed to be a good amount of very noisy activity a few hundred yards away. For a moment, I thought with dread that the Turks had arrived on our land. I asked an orderly what was going on, "We are destroying our weapons and our equipment so that Johnny can't get his hands on them. We have blown up our big guns and smashed our rifles. Look—you can see them over there."

A huge wooden chute leading to the river was being filled with all kinds of ammunition to render it useless. I saw some of our wagons being burnt—any material which could have been useful to the Turks was being destroyed. Officers were stamping on their compasses and field glasses and throwing their saddlery into the flames and were destroying their pistols and swords. Later, I heard an explosion and learnt that our wireless equipment had been destroyed. I wondered at the wisdom of doing this as the Turks would be furious and our negotiating position would be seriously weakened. I laid back and slept.

Later when I came to, I learned that Ned had already held private meetings with the Turks and had tried very hard to get the best terms for us. I wanted to talk to him and I asked the orderly to pass a message to him which he got just as he arrived back at Kut. He hurried over to the hospital barge. He was delighted to see me. I still felt awful and very weak, but I was determined to make a big effort despite my dire condition.

"How are you, old chap and how the hell did you come to be here?"

"Ned—I can't believe you made it at last. It's great to see you. I don't think I can talk very much but it will be great to listen to you and hear how you are getting on."

"First, please tell me, old friend, how you are and what's been happening here?"

I told him and gave him a summary of our situation. Much of it he already knew. I was truly delighted to see him as we had become such good friends when we worked together some years ago. He was a very intelligent and interesting chap, full of knowledge about the past and of the present of this fascinating land. I still felt dreadful but made a big effort to stay awake and alert. I told him about our general and asked him how he was cooperating.

"He's not too happy about us being here. He thinks my mission is dishonourable for a soldier like me. I told him that I'm not a soldier and that he doesn't yet know what my mission is. We didn't get off to a good start!"

"Unfortunately, I got here too late. There can only be one outcome now. We will be forced to surrender and that is not a good option but under the circumstances, it is the only one. We could have bought more time if say eight more biplanes had been sent with bags of food. If we had sent these, we would have been able to drop tons of food in the right places. The Germans could not have prevented this. We would, of course, have needed dozens of sorties over this small strip of land, but it could have been done. Our forces could have relieved Kut within three weeks."

He went on, "With more time, we could have fostered relationships with our friendlier local Arabs, some of whom are ready and able to rebel against the Ottomans, and we could have cut off their lines of supply from Baghdad. The Ottomans would have been as badly off as you are now. You will know about the incredible work Gerald has been doing in gaining support from the Arabs and supplying our troops but we British are disliked in this part of the world and this shouldn't be the case, but our reputation has now been further damaged by the humiliation of Kut. We can only win this war with the help of the locals and I intend to work with them to get their cooperation, but we must keep our promises to them and let them rule their land after the war is over. I am sorry to say that there are moves afoot to carve up their land for Europeans to enjoy and benefit from, but this is not our land—it's theirs and we must respect this. We should print our promises to these indigenous people and pin large notices up in every market place in this country informing them of our promises and then we could get their support. I feel more at home with the Arabs than I do with my own people. I believe I understand them and sometimes feel an affinity with them. I will fight with the Arabs and after the war, I will campaign for them against alien forces from within our own country."

He went on, "Gerald has been busy gaining support but also punishing Arabs who have been disloyal. Many of them have been looting our supplies and attacking isolated groups of soldiers. Incidentally, did you know that he led our group here and took us to the Turks? I hope he will be able to visit you, but I doubt it. He will be needed to lead us back. I hope to work with him after this in our efforts to defeat the Turks."

"I believe that we can motivate and mobilise the Arabs to fight with us and indeed it's a scandal that we haven't done more of this already and given support to people like Gerald. This will be the most shameful episode of British history when we capitulate to the Turks. The British public just won't believe it especially coming so soon after our failure in Gallipoli and there will be the most senior enquiry within our government. When we have posted our written promises to the Arabs across the country, there can be no shifting room after the war. We must keep our promises to them, but I am afraid that we may not. I will need to go back to the Turkish camp soon and I may not come back to Kut. You know that I will do my best for you all: I am going to try to get permission for all wounded to be allowed to go back to Basra. It won't be ideal but at least it will be better than being imprisoned by the Turks. I am sure you will be safe, but the journey won't be easy or comfortable. I don't trust the Turkish promises that all our men will be looked after and cared for. I believe that the reverse will be the case but there is nothing more I can do. Anything will be preferable to the fate of those who will be taken to Anatolia. For the release of our sick men to happen we will of course need to agree to let go thousands of Turkish prisoners," he went on.

"We should have carried out the Alexandretta project," he reflected.

"I've never heard of that—what was it?" I asked.

"Well, it was our idea to cut off the Turk's supply and eventually cause their advances to Palestine and Mesopotamia to collapse. The plan was to send a naval force carrying an army up the Mediterranean coast to land at the natural harbour at Alexandretta in Syria. We could have cut off all their forms of communication. Their railway network is centred there together with their main supply road. We could have stopped the flow of all essential supplies including men to the war zones and we would have forced them to their knees. We could have stopped thousands of troops coming from Gallipoli to strengthen their armies in the East and in addition, we could have fomented an Arab uprising against the Turks. It was such a simple plan and could have been extremely successful. I supported the plan along with several colleagues and senior generals and we developed the project in Cairo in fine detail over several months. It was a crushing blow to us when the Foreign Office shelved our plans."

"How many men would have been required for success?" I asked or rather rasped. I hadn't heard of this idea before, but it sounded practical and brilliant.

"We thought about one hundred to one hundred and fifty thousand men—it sounds a lot, but we could have found them and implemented the plan in weeks. Well, it was a huge risk and very daring but I'm sure it could have worked. It was surely worth a try to end both campaigns."

"Why didn't it go ahead?" I asked.

"Well, two reasons really: we got such a big bloody nose in Gallipoli and our politicians are still reeling from the shock and embarrassment—not to mention the huge losses of our men and those of our ANZAC allies. Our naval landings had failed miserably and there wasn't the will to repeat the exercise. Mesopotamia was beginning to stall and things were not exactly going well in Palestine and few had the bottle to risk it. Just imagine if it had gone the way of Gallipoli, the whole cabinet would have had to resign and military heads would have rolled."

"So, it was just fear of failure, was it? Hardly a good reason not to try out such a brilliant plan," I suggested.

"Well, it was the French who finally knocked this plan on its head. There was no way they were going to risk their nearby investments and territories—we wouldn't stand up to them. I sometimes consider who the biggest threat to our country is, and the French come first every time. I am extremely fearful of their plans when the war is over—after we have won it of course— there is no doubt at all in my mind that we will, but I fear that our promises to these indigenous people will not be honoured— we will roll over for the French. They have investments across the area and want to own the territories and turn them into French outposts, whereas our approach is to be much more hands off and let the people rule their own lands."

He was silent for a while and then went on in a softer tone, "I remember so well our venture in Sinai as one of the best times of my life and I would love to chat to you and recall those happy memories, we had a really good time there and at Carchemish."

"Yes. It was a wonderful time and I learned so much from you and Woolley about your archaeological dig and about the great battle between Pharaoh and Nebuchadnezzar. Your Arab friends were the best of company and looked after us so well," I recalled.

"Do you remember when the Germans were building that bridge for their Baghdad railway and they reneged on the agreed payments to their Arab workforce. They thought they could save some money by making them work and then wouldn't pay them at all. Well, what a mistake that was! It was the closest I have ever been to being shot—not once but at least ten times! But my goodness, the risks you took. You just charged at them screaming like a constipated dervish—I am relieved and surprised you are still with us—just!"

"Well, we managed to calm the situation down before many more were killed. Hopefully, the Germans learned a lesson but somehow, I doubt it," I added.

"I must go now. I need to continue our negotiations with the Turks. We must get you out of here to safety where you will be cared for and nursed back to health. Get well and keep safe, my good friend."

I was now exhausted after making the great effort to stay awake and talk although I was so pleased to be able to. This had been such a pleasant interlude after the hell we had all been through. I fell back onto my uncomfortable bed and slept once again.

Later, we heard that Ned and Townshend had offered the Turks one million pounds in gold to allow our whole army to escape south and when this was refused the offer was doubled. This was also refused but Ned did manage to negotiate safe passage for us wounded by agreeing to return Turkish prisoners. When the surrender finally came, they sent a Turkish medical officer to decide who was sick enough to be transported south by barge and those who would be fit enough to march with the others. I watched as this severe man with a black moustache and spectacles walked along our rows of beds. He pointed at me and I understood I would be sent south: many more would have to go with the Turks. I felt sorry for so many of these sick men. I was one of the lucky ones.

Lawrence was promised by the Turkish leaders that all other soldiers would be treated well and with great respect in captivity. This was one of the biggest lies ever told.

When Townshend finally surrendered on 29th April after holding out for almost five months, he thought himself to be the greatest military hero since Napoleon and the enemy treated him accordingly. I always knew he would walk all over us if he could gain glory and make his name in history.

The last the men saw of him he was being taken by motor boat towards Baghdad. We also heard that the Turks sent his yapping dog back to England. All our other men were to join a march through Mesopotamia all the way to prison camp in Turkey. They were promised safe passage by the Turks.

When the Turks charged into the town, they seized two hundred and fifty of the townsmen who they suspected of supporting us against them. They brought in tripods and hanged some and shot many others.

What happened to our men was one of most shameful scandals of the last few hundred years. Never had a captured army been treated in such a terrible and violent way by their captors. The men were beaten and occasionally gang raped by the Turks and by their Arab guards. They were fed old and dried biscuits which caused enteritis, and many died. They were forced to march many miles whilst being deprived of water and food. Many staggered bare-footed as their boots had been sold in exchange for a small amount of milk or they had been stolen from them. It still makes my blood boil to think of all our poor men suffering in this way. They were force-marched all the way into Anatolia and used as slave labour. They were fed very little; many did not have the strength to carry out the arduous work and many collapsed and died. And what food they were given was poor and it was not enough to sustain them. Most of them died and it is to our eternal shame that no one has ever been held accountable for this terrible treatment and genocide of our men.

Our officers were a lot more fortunate and were taken by barge to several prison camps where they were kept until the end of the war and although conditions were tough they were not made to work. Their worst suffering was terrible boredom during their two years of incarceration.

Meanwhile, Townshend enjoyed a comfortable imprisonment for the rest of the war in luxurious surroundings near Istanbul courtesy of the Turkish nation. He was never held to account for his actions believing that he had carried out a heroic and clever act. He had many opportunities to speak out in support of our poor soldiers and challenge the Turkish leaders. Fortunately, he never held a command or high office ever again. I sincerely hope he and I don't meet again for his sake.

I maintain to this day that we could have avoided the surrender of Kut and the many unnecessary deaths and suffering of the prisoners and the thousands of casualties who were sent to relieve us. It has been very painful to talk about this and I don't want to do so ever again. I hope one day I can forget this, but I fear that the memories are just too painful.

Herbert and Gerald:
Supplying the Army

You Lazarushian-leather Gunga Din!
Though I've belted you and flayed you,
By the livin' Gawd that made you,
You're a better man than I am, Gunga Din!

Rudyard Kipling

Gerald and I moved forward to meet the shaik and his guards to discover the truth about a vicious Arab attack on our forces. We knew damned well who was responsible, but Gerald wanted them to answer the accusations and lie if they dared to.

"Which of you butchered our men?" he roared. He repeated this again in their own language.

The group of about thirty moved towards us and at the last moment raised their rifles towards Gerald. They looked nervous as they tried to aim their guns but as he knew only too well they were very bad shots and their guns were pointed in just about every direction, some too close for comfort to both of us. I glanced quickly at Gerald and he was moving forward resolutely without any apparent fear. How could he do this while advancing into terrible danger? Surely, he must be afraid—any human being would be—but Gerald seemed to be different from others? I muttered some prayers believing that these were our last few moments on earth and said goodbye to my loved ones.

In response to their advance, he drew out his knobkerrie from his belt which he always carried with him and, ignoring the almost certain death from their rifles, he walked towards them bellowing obscenities and swung his weapon with brutal force. I shouted out to him that we were almost certain to be killed and that we should run for it. He ignored my protest and moved forward to smash heads and break bones causing devastation amongst the bewildered mob. A few shots were fired but in moments, the mob realised they were being outmanned, they turned and ran from the mad Englishman. The shots felt like a dozen buzzing bees speeding past my head and body but miraculously, I wasn't hit and could see that Gerald was unhurt, as well. He ran after them still roaring and yelling, threatening them with all kinds of violence and calling them the most terrible names, insulting their manhood, voicing accusations of sexual deviation and insulting their God. Miraculously, he was unharmed but had left a trail of broken bodies and whimpering souls. Those still able to move had run out of sight.

I felt very drained and relieved that we had both survived. I collapsed down and held my head in my hands, wiping the perspiration from my face. My hands were shaking with fear and relief: I looked up at Gerald, looking calm but muttering in his deep voice, "Just shows how guilty the bastards were. We taught them a bloody good lesson. The sodding buggers will think twice about attacking our men again. Medieval blasted butchers!" He yelled out to the vanishing mob, "Just in case you have any doubts this is Litma (this was the name they called him). Next time I'll chop your bloody balls off!"

This was the way he dealt with these people and dispensed justice. To him this was better than a court of law. He rarely killed in these circumstances, but he had the power to change minds and loyalties and this was his way of enforcing discipline. This was tough law enforcement—far away from any kind of law court and democracy, and very different from the latest ideas being promoted by the young upcoming political officers freshly out of military colleges. This was his opinion of them:

"Bloody drips and weaklings—all of them. They and their pussy doctrines will destroy our ambitions for these lands and bring the downfall of our empire. The way they are going we will have to give India back to the natives! Can you imagine the chaos that will bring? They will spend their time fighting each other in holy wars."

Gerald was fond of giving his views particularly after a good mess dinner and some strong Scotch whisky. Now, he was in full flow.

"They will destroy all the wealth and structure we have created. They will reverse hundreds of years of civilisation we have brought them. Where do these blue-eyed, milksop breast-sucking farts get their dangerous ideas from? I blame the red, knock-kneed pricks who teach them in schools and universities. Have you met that Gertrude Bell woman who is almost in charge over here? She wants to give the rabble independence. That's a short cut to a bloody revolution. We've got to keep ruddy control here; and we won't do it with appeasement."

When he got into his stride, there was no stopping him. Often, his audience included the young people he was describing, and they were mostly too afraid to disagree with him.

I returned to Mespot several times to bring the much-needed supplies to the army who were now winning their way through to Baghdad. I was ordered to give the army the best service and equipment I could after the shambolic episodes in the past when lack of supplies contributed to the earlier disasters of defeat and surrender. Our leaders were now determined to strengthen their campaign and smash the Ottomans back to where they came from.

Eddie had suggested that I contact Gerald who had helped the army so much in their previous campaign and had kept them supplied with essential consumables such as meat, vegetables, fruit and flour. He was able to source sheep, camels, mules and some horses. I decided to travel up the Tigris to meet him and to coordinate supplies; I was already bringing volumes of equipment and livestock from India, but I was sure we could do a better job working together. I met him in his office in Falahiyah just short distance from Kut. He called it an office but in truth, it was little better than a wooden shack. He had two Indian boys there, one who acted as his servant and the other as secretary.

The shack was peppered with bullet holes from the many times his Arab enemies had tried to assassinate him. There was a constant stream of visitors to his office, men, women and children who brought valuable information for which they were paid a few coins or a bag of sweets. On one occasion while I was there, two reporters came to the office and spent hours trying to persuade him to cooperate with publicity. One wanted to write a book about him and the other begged to pose for photographs. Gerald was having none of it and roughly pushed them away.

"Bloody reporters—you never know what the buggers are going to say about you. They make most of their stories up and before you know it, the knives are out for you. I've had dozens of these shitheads after me for years. I tell them all to fuck off back to their brothels."

I always have an image of how someone will look before I meet them for the first time. Gerald was quite different from what I expected. He was taller and very thin, and his skin was an unhealthy yellow colour and although I wasn't a doctor, I could see that he badly needed rest, preferably a year off back in the cool climate of England. I guessed he was suffering from several kinds of ailments and probably needed special treatment and an operation or two. He was not yet forty but looked many years older. Later when I suggested that he should take things easier, he acknowledged that this would make good sense, but the task was even bigger and more important now and without him the supply structure and British Arab cooperation could collapse. There was no one he could trust to take over his essential duties and he knew more about Arabia than anyone alive. He had a nervous twitch in his cheek and was constantly looking around him which probably, under the circumstances, was not surprising.

Later, he admitted that he suffered terrible stomach pains and could not remember when he had a good night's sleep. But my goodness, he was tough: he wasn't afraid of anyone and would stand up to generals and shaiks and made plenty of enemies of both. He disrespected most of his senior officers, at least until they had proved their cleverness or courage to him, but they had now made him full colonel. He had travelled to some of the most inhospitable parts of the world with scant supplies and often little water. I don't think he knew what fear was. He was either loved or hated by people, but all greatly respected him. Sometime later, he returned to England where he spent many months in hospital: his appendix was removed, and the surgeons were amazed that he had kept going in his state of health. They had never seen a case like this before.

Gerald was dressed in filthy Arab clothes and with his dark skin and mannerisms, he was taken for a Bedouin tribesman. He could speak all the local languages and knew the dialects. He even smelled like a Bedouin and could easily join a group of them and be fully accepted. He only wore his army uniform when he was meeting his peers.

I was fascinated to learn how he worked. His methods were completely unorthodox but ultimately very successful. If he had worked by the book and never-ending regulations, he would have achieved very little. The expression to take the bull by the horns could have been made for him. A story I heard about him much later completely changed my opinion about him: he was storming an Arab building when he threw a bomb largely destroying it and unfortunately, a young boy was killed in the explosion. Weeks later, he was told that the mother of the boy was in a deep depression and Gerald visited her. He was very remorseful and gave her some money from his own account and revisited her at intervals to give her presents and more money and he kept this up for as long as he could. Everyone had a story about Gerald and his exploits were legendary.

The Arab attack which he had beaten off had taken place just the second day after I had met him. We had driven in his 'Avenger' which was a heavily armoured car. These days he only used horses and camels on rare occasions. Now, he travelled in vehicles which were powered by petrol. We boated across the river and drove about thirty miles to the offending Arabs.

Another day, we were cruising along the Tigris on a visit to another tribe. Gerald had acquired a Thames river cruiser and delighted in giving lifts to soldiers who waved and called out to him. It was an honour to travel with a man who they respected so much. The objective this time was to gather support from a group of Arabs to attack a Turkish airfield and destroy their planes. The shaik readily agreed to the venture and promised to lead twenty men to the place. They would set out immediately and meet with him at an agreed venue a short distance from the airfield. Gerald planned to drive to the venue in several days and would travel with the Arabs to achieve their objective. I was beginning to understand the enormous scope of his work.

"Want to come along for the Craic?"

I had to get back by the end of next month, so I had time to assist.

"How can I help with the expedition?" I asked.

Gerald asked me to gather the stores we would need for the next couple of weeks, including petrol and spare parts for the armoured car and we took along his two servants. We left a day later, it was extremely hot and so the breeze in our faces was very welcome. I had misgivings as we drove off, wondering if this was part of my duties or an opportunity for adventure. I convinced myself that this was for the common good; as soon as we could bring this war to an end the better. We met up with his group of Arabs at the agreed place and covered the short distance to the airfield. We stopped and surveyed the place through our field glasses. I saw about thirty German planes lined up on a mud runway and just beyond three wooden huts. I could also see about half a dozen guards standing around the planes. No doubt there were more soldiers and airman in the huts. We sat with our Arabs partners well hidden from the guards and Gerald divided the men into two groups. The shaik's men looked hardened and professional.

"This is what we are going to do," he explained, "you will approach the woods over there and launch a diversionary attack on the huts attack while the second group will destroy the aircraft with bullets and bombs. I will join you later."

"Where will you be?" one of them asked. Gerald pointed at one plane which was set slightly apart from the others. There were about thirty biplanes in total.

"I want that one. You mustn't damage it even a tiny bit. Anyone who does so will have me to answer to. I want it in perfect condition. Herbert—I want you to drive over there and tie the tail of that plane to the back of the car. Then tow it over here. I will lead the attack on the huts and we will keep the men away from the planes, so you will only have the few guards to deal with and you can concentrate on destroying the other planes. When we start the attack, I will blow a whistle which means you can get started. Any questions?"

It all seemed straightforward. I had to move forward first so I drove off to Gerald's plane. I seemed to be making a terrific din and in no time at all two of the guards were running towards me and firing. As the bullets pinged off the metal sides, I suddenly felt alone and exposed, but I focused on where I was going without being distracted. I had been in a few skirmishes before but nothing like as many as Gerald. I had learnt in war that you just had to get on with the job you were given and try to ignore the ever-present dangers. I got to the plane and reversed up to the tail and started to open the door to get out and do my job, but the two guards were close now and more were joining them. I could almost hear Gerald saying, "Get your bloody big arse out of the car and tie the fucking tail up." So, that is exactly what I did; as I opened the door and stood up, the guards were close now and had the easiest target. The next shot whistled over my shoulder: I took out my pistol and shot the nearest man and he fell. The other man had a clear shot as I scampered round to the back of the car to get the rope. A shot rang out and the second man slammed to the dust. Unknown to me, Gerald had run forward to keep an eye on me.

"Get on with it—tie the bloody tail up! I'm meant to be with the others over there."

And with that he charged forward to join those attacking the hut. I did my job as fast as I could, got back in the car and gently moved forward as the plane bobbed along behind me as I drove to where he had told me to. I looked over to see how the attack was going and things didn't look good. The planes were mostly on fire or in bits, but the attack on the huts was not going well; a swarm of men rushed out firing at Gerald's men as he was running forward to catch up after assisting me. There must have been two hundred of them: our men were hopelessly outnumbered and beginning to waver. Gerald charged forward screaming at the top of his voice firing in all direction, while lobbing grenades into the thick of the men. His extreme bravado inspired his men to move forward again and, in that moment, I briefly wondered if he had a death wish with his utter recklessness.

The battle was terrible and in the end Gerald's men got the advantage as the enemy retreated but our losses were very bad. Of Gerald's group only three men were left standing and overall, we had suffered fifty per cent casualties. However, our Arabs could see that the battle had been won and ran forwards whooping and shouting while butchering the retreating enemy. No one was spared in this horrible slaughter and the Arabs were victorious. I was horrified by the violence but realised there was no use in protesting to Gerald. I had to admit that his brutal methods were very effective in this awful war.

The whole venture was going to cost Gerald a lot of valuable silver in payment and compensation which he had agreed beforehand with the Arab group, but the objective had been achieved. As I drove back towing his precious cargo behind us bobbing and swaying, he ordered me to go slowly and carefully. Gerald went very quiet and fell into a deep sleep. I wondered what was wrong and then noticed blood on his left thigh. I stopped the car to have a better look at the wound. A bullet had passed through the fleshy part and I knew I had to put tight bandages around his leg to stop the blood flow. I treated him immediately despite his loud and very rude protests. We got back safely a few hours later extremely tired but with his beautiful prize intact.

****

On my next visit a few months later, he took me up for my first flight. He had painted the plane a dark red colour for some reason and beneath each wing was a very good painting of a rampant lion, probably to enhance his image and frighten his enemies. I sat in the seat at the back and wondered if I had made a terrible mistake. His servant swung the propeller and the engine roared into noisy power and swamped me with smelly fumes. We moved at a terrific pace, bumping and creaking and soared up into the air, climbing to a dizzy height and then levelling off. We followed the Tigris south and I marvelled at the twisting river with its swaying palms. I could see miles of dusty plains and huge mountains into the distance. I never imagined it would be anything like this and thrilled at the experience.

The noise of the engine with the wind ripping past my head precluded any talking. Gerald pointed towards the mountains west of the river indicating that we would be flying in that direction. We looked down and saw some of our soldiers camped below and they all came out of their tents and waved at us. They all knew Gerald and wanted to give their thanks for all the support he was giving them. Now, I could see that we were following the Euphrates and later, he pointed downwards. He had told me earlier that we would be flying over ancient Babylon and as I followed his arm I looked down. I was sorry that there was now little evidence of this once magnificent ancient city. We were off to visit one of the Muntafiq tribes and this time a peaceful one. We were negotiating the supply of five thousand sheep for our army which had recently taken Baghdad. The new force now led by our British commanders had charged up the Tigris and had defeated the Turks in numerous encounters without any setbacks.

I was intrigued to witness the negotiations with the shaik after we bumped down the dusty track landing safely. The tribe rode to meet us and gave us camels to travel the last few miles to their camp. As we sat around with the group, compliments were exchanged, and refreshments were offered. This went on for so long that I wondered if we would ever get around to business. I did not understand the language, but the meaning was clear. At one stage, I thought they were going to murder us as the exchanges got so heated, but Gerard had prepared me for the meeting and explained it was quite normal practice. At a later stage, I gathered that the price was being discussed and the tempo rose once again. Later, Gerard explained to me that he insisted on accompanying the tribe with the sheep to Baghdad just to make sure that the deal was honoured. He also wanted to see them delivered in good health. Eventually, the deal was done, and we parted with hugs and handshakes promising lifelong love, honour and devotion to all.

Overall, I made three trips to meet with Gerald. We managed to coordinate our work and made tremendous progress giving efficient and timely supply to our victorious army. We made a vast improvement in the supply of medical equipment and I was informed that there were no shortages anywhere. In addition, more doctors and nurses were sent to the front and our men had much better care, saving many more lives. The hospital in Basra was fully operational now having been fully refurbished and repaired. The arrival of dozens of Queen Alexandra's nurses had ensured high standards were reached and maintained. There was little need for me to take the wounded to India any more.

Gerald and I struck up a good friendship and although I didn't like some of his methods, I had to admit that his approach was very successful, and he achieved more than anyone else. We had many hours to talk and I heard that his career started in the Boer War as mine had. We exchanged many stories and experiences of that terrible campaign—well, all campaigns were terrible. There are no good wars, and few achieved anything good in the long term: well, certainly not in Arabia as we were to find out years later. We had lit a fuse which had caused never-ending eruptions over many years.

Gerald had started his political work in the early part of the century just a few years after the end of the Boer War. He arrived in India and travelled to many parts of the country particularly to the mountains in the north. His work took him to many parts of the globe including all parts of the Ottoman Empire, Afghanistan, Bulgaria, Russia and many more; and of course, to all parts of Arabia. He met with all the powerful men in the south and tried to persuade them to the British cause. He was instrumental in getting support from Ibn Saud and Faisal who, together with their sons, would become the most powerful Arabian leaders of the future.

After the war was over, Gerald faced a further challenge when he found himself in the middle of the Arab revolt. This was a huge and unexpected development and cost our country very dearly in precious lives and resources. Most people have forgotten these dire times and recent history has tended to airbrush the awful crisis.

Amicia: Travelling to India

The life that I have
Is all that I have
And the life that I have
Is yours.
The love that I have
Of the life that I have
Is yours and yours and yours.
A sleep I shall have
A rest I shall have
Yet death will be but a pause.
For the peace of my years
In the long green grass
Will be yours and yours and yours.

Leo Marks

When the letter arrived at our house, I was in the kitchen preparing dinner for my father, the Reverend Edmund Manwaring-White. He had been the rector at St Mary's Mendlesham for many years as had his father before him. He had been educated at Cambridge and kept hundreds of books in his large study where he would spend several hours each evening. His special interest was the history of the Civil War and he was hugely proud of a small museum which he looked after in his church. He would only let a favoured few through the locked door into the small room on a mezzanine floor and they would marvel at the few dozen weapons and armour of the Civil War and the highly polished furniture of the period. He would spend hours cleaning and maintaining these precious artefacts.

I lived at home at the huge vicarage in several acres of wooded grounds and looked after him together with my dear sister, Marianne, better known as Kitty. As children, we loved to play in this magical area with a small pond in the centre. To us, it looked like a huge lake and indeed we were told it was called the 'Shark Lake'—I think to make sure we kept away from it! Years later, I also told my own children to stay away from the Shark Lake. Yes, we had a very happy childhood and I was always close to my family and would do anything to help them.

I worked as a nurse in nearby Bury St Edmunds but returned home most nights to look after him. If I had to work the night shift, Kitty was often there to cook and care for him. During the day, she worked part time as an ambulance driver which she was very good at but only when she concentrated but this was on rare occasions only. She loved to talk and when she did, she had to look at the people she was talking to; whilst driving this was to the passengers in the front seat and indeed she could not resist turning around and doing the same with the patients in the back!

Our mother had died some years before and while father was in sound body and mind he was still looking after the church and his parish. We all got on very well although he could be very obstinate and cantankerous at times, but we knew that he became tired after long days doing his duties and often suffered difficult parishioners.

Kitty was now engaged to be married and she was spending less time at the house. She was going to marry a local clergyman and she couldn't wait for the day to come. As for me, I wondered if I would ever find the right man. Yes, there had been a few boyfriends but nothing too serious, well perhaps a doctor at the hospital, but he had moved away now, and it was difficult to keep in touch across a large distance. I desperately wanted a family of my own, but time was passing by and to my horror, it looked like I was to be left on the shelf just like a lonely maiden aunt of mine. I was fast approaching that age when the opportunity to produce children became less likely. I used to imagine my future husband and three children and even had names for them all. Fortunately, I was kept very busy with my work and had little time to daydream. Mostly, it was only father and I in the big draughty house and it was very lonely, particularly on chilly winter nights. Our elder brothers had long since left the family home: one became a doctor in London and the other was abroad in the army.

I heard the clunk of the rusty flap as the postman pushed a letter through the front door. Letters were quite frequent, so I went to fetch it in no great hurry. As I stooped to pick it up, I could see from the stamp and the envelope markings that the letter had come from India which was a mystery. The only person I knew in India was my brother, Eddie, but he was away in Mesopotamia fighting the Ottomans in the war. Of course, we had all read about Kut and the awful surrender by the British and we were all worried about Eddie who had been in the country for around a year, but specific news was rare and sporadic. I opened it in trepidation and as I unfolded and read the letter, my feeling was one of great concern and blessed relief. I called out to my father in the drawing room:

"Father—Eddie is in India wounded!"

"What—how bad is he?"

"I don't know but he's asked me to go out there to look after him. It must be quite bad. Oh, the poor boy! I must go immediately."

The expected reply quickly came back from him immediately, "Of course—that is quite out of the question. There's a war on don't you know!"

And so, it was a week later that I boarded a steamship at Southampton heading towards Bombay. I clearly remember all the troops walking up the gangplanks and the huge cranes swinging over the ship loading the cargo. Above all, I remember the deafening noise: a brass band, the clanking of machinery and shouts of the crowd to their sons, brothers and husbands. The men all waved and yelled, much louder when they recognised their families.

I was the only female on the ship which was carrying soldiers to India for training before travelling to Mesopotamia to boost our war effort there. They were all aware that we had had a terrible setback with the surrender at Kut and our government was now determined to gain the initiative and push the Turks back to where they came from.

I managed to get a private cabin, thank goodness, and the ship's crew brought me basic food—enough to keep me alive. I had to share the toilet arrangements with the men, which was horrible, particularly with the onset of sea sickness, both theirs and mine. The cabin was very hot and stuffy and so I climbed up to the open deck to breathe clean fresh air as often as I could, but the decks were so crowded I could hardly move about. There wasn't enough room down below for all the men and so hundreds of them stayed on the deck. One of the men told me that the ship had taken on board far too many: he told me that there were around three thousand men on board on a nine-thousand-tonne ship which should have carried no more than fifteen hundred. They all dreaded being hit by a U-Boat and there were not enough lifeboats for so many. They all complained that they weren't being given enough to eat and indeed they were forced to pay an extortionate amount to the crew for basic bread and butter.

It seemed extraordinary to me that we called up these thousands of men to war, took them to the other side of the world and didn't even give them enough food to eat. Two of the men died before we got to India, and the men and I believed that this was from lack of nourishment and starvation. I hoped things improved for the men in India and I asked one of them, a very gentle young man called Daniel, to write to me in Simla to let me know how they were doing. I told him I was going to look after my brother who had been badly injured at Kut. Daniel said that many of their friends from the same regiment were killed while trying to relieve the men at Kut and they were determined to avenge them.

"There's a mad feeling among us. We can't wait to get at the devils."

Daniel said they were all being sent to a place in the north which he said was called Quetta. They were staying at Clive Barracks. They were being trained and prepared for their visit to the Gulf which was due to start in a couple of months. His biggest concern was leaving behind his beloved sister, Maud, in England as he was very close to her and he worried about her all the time. He said he was going to write to her as often as he could. All the men were very polite and respectful to me and I had no trouble at all during the journey.

Daniel told me that we were approaching the Bay of Biscay and to prepare for choppy waters. I didn't appreciate then the soldiers' humour of extreme understatement. We rolled, dipped and dived through the waters to such an extent that I thought the boat would tip over, projecting the hundreds of men on top into the swirling sea. Eventually, we sailed through these waters into the calm of the Mediterranean and the weather became hotter in the daytime and all of us tried to squeeze on to the deck to cool off. It was stifling below decks.

"How did you get permission to travel in wartime?" Daniel asked me one day.

"Well, it wasn't easy; my father is a clergyman and he spoke to dozens of people, even to the Archbishop, but eventually, a general in Eddie's regiment made arrangements."

There was a condition though: I had to join Queen Alexandra's Military Nursing Service for India. This means that I should nurse wounded soldiers and I would have to attend Naini Tal College for specialised training some way from Simla. The benefit was that the passage was paid for and I was to receive a small salary, and this was important as I had no independent means. Fortunately, I qualified as I was single and over twenty-five although this condition was being eased due to the pressures of war. I was actually very pleased to be joining as the advantages were many—including being paid a small wage—and I would still be able to see and look after Eddie every day.

I also told Daniel about Kitty and how helpful she had been by postponing her wedding to look after Father. I told him that just like him, I would do anything for my family who I loved dearly. Daniel had a kind and caring heart and I became very fond of him.

Daniel and his friends then told me about the threat of U-Boats as we came near to Egypt. Many of their friends had been swallowed up by the sea after being torpedoed some months ago. One ship went down not far from Port Said and our ship zigzagged to try to avoid the U-Boats patrolling the seas. Later, we spotted a bigger ship overtaking us and someone saw a U-Boat following us a couple of miles away: we were all extremely worried.

We all stood on deck as the alarm sounded and lifebelts were handed out row by row although there weren't enough for everyone. When the alarm stopped there was a deathly silence and all the men stood in line stoically and no one panicked even though we were all possibly facing a horrible death. I heard Daniel praying quietly, mentioning his sister's name and other members of his family. Everyone stood very still, and we could only hear the ship's engines; not a word was spoken. I had never been so close to death before and I closed my eyes tightly and repeated some of my father's prayers. I was certain we were going to die, and I prayed that it would happen quickly and painlessly.

I was very frightened and then I realised all the men were just as scared and I felt it was my duty to be brave and to show a good example. I looked around me and smiled confidently at all the pale faces. After a very tense few minutes, it seemed that we were not to be the target today as the U-Boat overtook us and followed the other ship which was some miles ahead of us. Within forty-five minutes, we saw and heard the terrible explosion as the target ship was hit: the flames and smoke streamed skywards and later, the sea all around us was filled with thousands of scraps of wood and debris. I felt so sorry for all the poor men and their families, but I still said a prayer thanking Him for our survival.

Well, my father had warned me of the dangers of travelling to India in wartime and as a single woman, as well. It had taken me only twenty-four hours to convince him that I could not let Eddie down and it was my Christian duty to go to him. Well, that struck home as my father preached Christian duty to his parishioners and family constantly!

"I heard you mention the name Nellie. Who is she?" I asked Daniel.

"She's my girl—she's the best girl I have ever had, and she looked after me so well when I was with her in Bournemouth. Well, actually, I hope she will be my girl if I come back safe and sound. I shall stick to her for I know she's worth it."

I asked him how he felt during the tense moments of danger on the deck.

"I stood face to face with God."

Months later, I received a letter from Daniel who was now in the Kitchener Barracks in Quetta. It seems that the men were still not being fed properly and had to supplement their diet out of their wages. They were based in the far north of the country close to Afghanistan, near to a mountain pass where they were constantly plagued by men from the hill tribes. Tribesmen used to sneak in at night to steal anything useful they could get their hands on. Daniel's rifle was stolen one night, and he was in big trouble the next day. They were undergoing intense training in preparation for their move to the Gulf which was due just days from now. Daniel said that they could not wait to get there to avenge their friends. I was amazed at their determination: Daniel had told me about the strong team spirit and their immense pride in the regiment. Above all, they looked out for each other before considerations of their own safety. Their mates were the most important people in the world. This was the driving force of the British Army and had been for centuries. I guessed that by the time I received his letter, they had already arrived there.

Sadly, I learnt many months later that Daniel had been killed in one of the many battles which our army fought advancing northwards up the Tigris towards Baghdad. I cried tears for him and his poor family and hoped he didn't suffer too much. Here was a man so full of love for his family and friends: a good man who was a true Christian. I was so sad for him and the millions of men and their families all over the world who had suffered in this terrible war. Daniel was buried at the Amara Cemetery near the Tigris in Mesopotamia.

We travelled safely through the Suez Canal and around the huge landmass of Arabia and apart from incessant heat, I was all right. I couldn't wait to get to India and to travel north to see my brother. We felt the fierce heat first and then saw the Bombay debris and flotsam in the sea and eventually, the brown line of the Indian coast loomed into view with the city buildings and the bustling docks. It was such as relief to get here at last.

I was left alone at the docks in Bombay after the men had disembarked and marched off and I was unsure of how to get to the station. I had said goodbye to Daniel and his friends and we promised to keep in touch. Looking around, I wondered at the heat, the flies, the smells, the musky steamy air and the noise of India, the bustle of a big city with many thousands of people frantically going about their business and fell deeply in lifelong love with the country. This love affair continues to this day long after we had left the continent with little chance we would ever return.

A boy with a rickshaw walked up to me jabbering in a strange language. He was dressed in dirty rags and showed a toothless mouth as he opened it to speak. I couldn't understand him and so I said train station in a clear voice. In moments, I was transported away and was pleased I had managed the next stage in my journey.

Within a few hours, I was travelling in a crowded train heading north towards Simla. There were no seats available but fortunately, a smart young gentleman stood up and offered his window seat to me. I was extremely tired, so it was a blessed relief. I thanked him profusely and sat back to admire the fascinating and varied scenery, huge dusty plains and later, stunning mountains. I was surprised at the immensity of the country as I had never been out of England before and all these experiences were exciting and new. Later, the same gentleman offered me some very welcome food and water.

It was such a long journey and we had to change trains several times with long pauses in between. At one station, local boys brought us some delicious tea and sweets and at another, we had hot food on the platform. I walked up and down to ease my inactive limbs and then reached up to open the train door. I screamed as the metal brass handle scorched my hand and pulled it away quickly. The kind gentleman took out a handkerchief and opened the door for me. Later, he soothed my burn with a cool cream. I was slowly being seduced by this magnificent country, absorbing the hot spicy air and the delicious flavours but most of all, I fell in love with the kind and gentle people.

At last, after four days, we climbed on the final train and were told that Simla was now only sixty miles away. I couldn't wait to get there now and assumed we would be there in an hour or two, but I hadn't allowed for the approaching Himalayas: It was a huge climb of more than four thousand feet crossing huge passes and going over innumerable bridges and through long tunnels. One of the bends was terrifying: as we turned sharply to the left, I looked out of the window and straight down the side of a mountain and the ground was so far away the land was completely out of sight. To make matters worse, the train was leaning over towards the open space and I was convinced that we would tip over into the bottomless void. I closed my eyes tightly and prayed intensely. I started with the Lord's prayer and appealed to every saint I could remember to implore them to save us. I opened my eyes and saw that we had survived, and we were now going through yet another tunnel. As the train climbed higher, the air became deliciously cold and fresh and we moved up to the top of the world. The sun was just setting over the huge mountains: I had never experienced scenery like this before and had not expected such a contrast of magnificence. I couldn't wait to see Eddie after so many years and wondered how he would be.

****

I awoke early morning as the bright warm sun streamed in through the window in my bungalow. I knew it was a special day but for a second, I couldn't remember why. Just then my maid, Geeta, knocked and came in with a welcome cup of tea. It was my wedding day of course and I was supremely happy. I sipped my tea and reflected to my arrival in this lovely country nearly four years ago. I looked out at our beautiful garden rustling in the early morning breeze in the bright sun already raising the temperature to uncomfortable levels. We had two peacocks strutting and squawking on the grass. There was a cacophony of noise as wild parrots were screeching and monkeys chattering. Later, they would come to my window and see what I was doing so they could copy my movements, but I kept my window closed tightly as I knew they would come in and steal my brushes and cosmetics—as one little fellow did a few weeks ago.

I looked at the banks of beautiful flowers: I loved the fuzz-buzz, roses of bright red, yellow and white, blue lavender, exotic lotus and orchids; so many varieties thrived in this climate. We also had dozens of fruit trees including fig and mango, but my favourites were the magnificent rhododendrons, but they needed intensive trimming and control, otherwise they spread wildly. In another part of the garden, we grew vegetables—many which we could grow in England such as cabbage, carrots and cauliflower but also more exotic varieties, okra and eggplant. I saw the gardener, Suresh, tirelessly tending to the beds, pulling out weeds and adding them to the bag which he slung over his shoulder.

I watched as Govinda, the milkman, led his cow towards the back gate and started milking her. I watched carefully just to make sure he didn't add any dirty water to the milk as many of them did. Some of our neighbours had become sick in this way. He then brought the fresh milk to the back door to be greeted by the cook.

I worked hard at my job at the hospital and we seemed to have a constant flow of wounded men from Mesopotamia, often more than we could handle. More of the wounded were getting better due to the care and attention, not to mention the supply of more good skilled doctors and the availability of drugs and medicines. I looked after Eddie almost every evening for over two years. I took Sundays off and walked to the bazaar with Geeta for the weekly shop. I loved the noise and the bustle with all the bright colours and the pushing crowds. The stalls had rows of herbs and spices and the air was full of hot musty aromas. There was an abundance of fruit and vegetables, but we tried to become self-sufficient with our garden produce. In the evening, I would return once more to look after Eddie. I never missed an evening.

****

I was thinking back to my first day in Simla: after the long and gruelling train journey, I was met at the station by a lieutenant colonel who introduced himself as Herbert. He was very polite and softly spoken and explained that he was responsible for taking the wounded men back to India from Mesopotamia. He had taken my wounded brother, Eddie, off a barge at Basra and told me that it was a miracle that he had survived and over the months that followed, the two men had become friends. I wondered what the two of them had in common but of course I was aware that friendships often develop between opposite characters.

Here was Herbert who was very quiet and rather shy and my brother, Eddie, noisy and loud. He could light up a room with his conversation and jokes and the loudest laughter which followed was invariably his. Friendships often occur when people share great adversity as they clearly had. I noticed that Herbert had very dark skin and wondered if he was part of the Anglo-Indian community but learned later that this was due to years exposed to the heat and fierce sun. I asked Herbert to describe how Eddie was.

"Well, he will tell you that nothing is wrong and that I had forced him to write to you. The fact is that he has been through a terrible ordeal—worse than any other soldier I know of—and

160

despite his bluster, his mind has been seriously affected. That is in addition to his physical condition and he is still very much weakened. He needs help to take his food and drink—and to be kept away from alcohol—only water and tea for him! Above all, he needs gentle attention for his mental condition. On the Western Front, they call it shell-shock, but this is more than that. I am sure he will fully recover with your assistance, but this will take months of care. He lost part of his jaw in the explosion and he will be scarred for life—not that he worries about such things. I will introduce you to his doctor who will give you much better professional diagnosis than I can."

On my way to the hospital, I was thinking about my dear brother, Eddie and the wonderful childhood we had enjoyed together. I was dearly fond of my three siblings, Eddie, Dicky and Kitty. There was nothing I wouldn't do for them and likewise, I know that their love was always returned in full.

When I was older, I was sent to stay with my uncle and aunt in Cheltenham where they ran a nursing home and he practised as a surgeon. They kindly paid for me to go to the Cheltenham Ladies College which I really enjoyed, and I made lifelong friends, one of whom I worked with in India on charitable projects. Alice Cohen was married to the Viceroy Lord Reading and they were both extremely generous with their time and money for those less fortunate. We organised a reception for the Prince of Wales who was to become Edward VIII when he visited India. He insisted on playing alongside the polo team, but it became apparent he wasn't a good enough rider and he kept falling off his horse. He was immensely charming though and blended in with our group seamlessly.

I cried when I first saw my dear brother looking pale and thin lying quietly on his bed. I saw the huge scar on the left side of his face and the permanent dent to his features. I gently hugged him, and he was trying to hold back the tears but was unsuccessful. We did not speak for a few minutes; words were not necessary. Later, he wanted to know all about my journey and the family news. He had not heard from Molly, his wife, for some time. She was still living with her family in Holland and was planning to travel to India when the war was over. I gave Eddie some soup and he was now ready to sleep. I was looking forward to caring for him and nursing him to better health both physically and mentally. I had had several years of nursing experience in Suffolk, in Stowmarket to be precise, and I had also volunteered for the Red Cross. I had tended many wounded men from the Western Front. When it was time to leave, Herbert took me to a comfortable bungalow which the regiment had very kindly provided for me.

I cared for Eddie for more than two years and he was making really good progress. I practised techniques I had learnt to relieve extreme stress and 'Shell Shock' as this was known. I had also heard this was called 'War Neurosis' and thousands of men coming back from the trenches were so afflicted. I had to develop a strong bond of trust with him which was not difficult between close siblings and used forms of psychotherapy; explanation, persuasion and suggestion together with massage and warm baths with light exercise. Plenty of rest was essential. I also encouraged him to take up his boyhood hobby of wood carving and he made lovely models of animals for me and the nurses.

Other wounded men also asked for models to send home to their children. Gradually, his natural bluster and good humour returned, and he kept the whole hospital entertained. His jokes were not suitable for female company, but I frequently heard him when I was out of sight and laughed at his stories, but mostly, I laughed because I was happy he was getting so much better. Eventually, he was ready to return to his regiment in Poona with a strong recommendation from his doctors that it was time for a desk job with no or limited stress. I was very sorry to see him go and we promised to visit each other as often as possible.

It was now time for me to go back home as my job was done and the war was almost over. However, I was growing very attached to Herbert and we saw each other every day at the hospital with Eddie. We had also dined together and had drinks in the officers' mess on many occasions. We also loved to look after his colourful garden and planted dozens of bright flowers, herbs and spices. When I first met him, I liked him immediately, but I never thought of him as a romantic partner. He just wasn't my type.

One day, it suddenly struck me that I wanted to see this man every day and couldn't live without him. I so admired Herbert; he was so quiet and gentle, and I couldn't fathom how he could command such a large group of men and staff at the regiment.

He was just too nice, and I never heard him once raise his voice. This was also a mystery to his fellow officers and a bit of a running joke but they all conceded that despite his mild disposition, he commanded profound respect. He treated everyone as equals including all the Indians regardless of their religion and caste. He would never get into an argument with me or indeed anyone else and if a disagreement came up, he would just go quiet on me. Herbert cared very deeply for animals and hated to see anyone being cruel to them. His horrible experiences in Mesopotamia where men and animals were mutilated caused him terrible anguish. When he recalled these sufferings, his manner changed abruptly, and he would become very loud and vocal against those who caused the sufferings. I fell deeply in love with him.

Herbert was seven years older than me at forty-five and we both agreed that we would love to have children, although we could not afford to wait too long, if, of course, we were so blessed. Herbert had a few more years of service in India to complete but intended to retire as soon as he could, and we would return to England. In the meantime, we would have to bring our children up in India. Most doctors considered that four years was the maximum that children should live in India due to the environment and climate. If necessary, I could take the children back to England on my own and this should be possible now that the war was over. However, one step at a time and it was perhaps unwise to plan too much in the future which was always impossible to predict.

We were now stationed a few miles further north in Murree which, if anything, was more beautiful than Simla and somewhat cooler. We were offered, for our wedding, the beautiful Holy Trinity Church built in the traditional English gothic style, far too large for our needs but lovely and cool in the hot summer. Our wedding day was planned for the 5th of July 1920 and as expected, it turned out to be a lovely balmy day with clear blue skies. We decided with the military chaplain there who readily agreed to preside at the service. As we drove to the church, I felt I was being treated like a member of the Royal Family. The chaplain was lovely and delivered a faultless service speaking in his rich deep voice.

Our reception was in the world famous Ahrans Restaurant where we had real champagne and food with the most gentle and delicious flavours. Yes, this was an extravagant treat, but it was well worth the expense. We wanted to get away from the officers' mess and the atmosphere of the military which we had to live with all the time. The colonel of the regiment lent us his magnificent and majestic Rolls Royce.

Just to make the day complete, my darling brother, Eddie and his wife, Molly, (who I had just met for the first time) were here to celebrate with us. Also attending were Ernest Cripps (Crispy to us his friends) and his wife, Esme. When I heard from Julia that Gerald and she would be coming, I cried with unashamed delight. Cousin Gerald was very dear to us and had had a horrible war in Mespot where he had served with incredible courage. Eddie and Herbert had often told me about his almost legendary exploits in Arabia over many years and how they had worked together.

Eddie and Mollie were always extremely grateful to me for caring for him so well for those two years. My care for him was only natural after all and it was my privilege to do so.

Crispy, Eddie and Herbert had fought for many years in tough campaigns and would remain close friends for the rest of their lives. My favourite picture is the one we had taken of our group outside the church and I look at it each day with great love and affection.

The bride and groom, Amicia and Herbert.
Eddy is top row, left.

Afterword

Amicia and Herbert were blessed with three children, Eve, Rosemary and Peter who became my dear father. Peter did not thrive in the Indian climate and environment and the doctor strongly recommended that he should be taken to the temperate climate of England. Amicia took her three children on the difficult journey back to England and her father took them in at the vicarage. The children fondly recalled the Shark Lake which they were warned to stay away from.

In 1926, Herbert retired from the Indian Army and came back to England to his family. He died at the early age of sixty in 1935 of kidney failure probably due to the poor quality of the food and water he consumed in Mesopotamia and the Indian environment with its extremities of weather. Amicia, my grandmother, lived on for another eighteen years. Unfortunately, I never got to meet Amicia and Herbert.

Gerald is a fictional character largely based on the legendary Gerard Leachman, who was killed in the Arab revolt days after he returned to Mespot, just one month after the wedding. He was visiting a shaik when his son and collaborators shot him in the back as he was leaving. Gerald was eventually buried in Baghdad with full military honours.

Crispy was my dutiful godfather. I also never met Uncle Eddie but my cousins, Judith and Michael, when they were young children, remember a tall monster of a man with an ugly scar on his face and a booming voice, standing at the doorway before entering their house. Judith was so scared of him that she hid in the cupboard under the stairs.

Bibliography

The Boer War, 1999, Tabitha Jackson. By Channel 4 Books, an imprint of Macmillan Publishers Ltd.

The Indian Army and the King's Enemies, 1900-1947, 1988, Charles Chenevix Trench, Thames and Hudson.

Eden to Armageddon: World War I in the Middle East, 2009, Roger Ford. Weidenfield & Nicolson, The Orion Publishing Group Ltd.

Enemy on the Euphrates, 2014, Ian Rutledge. Saqi Books.

Seven Pillars of Wisdom. A Triumph, 1922, T E Lawrence, Private Edition.

The Mistress of Abha, 2010, William Newton, Bloomsbury, USA.

Lawrence of Arabia: The Life, the Legend, 2005, Malcolm Brown, Thames and Hudson Ltd.

Lawrence of Arabia's War, 2016, Neil Faulkner. Yale University Press.

Forgotten Soldiers of the First World War, 2007, David R Woodward. Tempus Publishing ltd.

On the Psychology of Military Incompetence, 2011, M Dixon, Norman F Dixon. Random House.

Nebuchadrezzar and Babylon, 1985, D J Wiseman. Oxford University Press.

KUT 1916, 2009, Patrick Crowley, by Spellmount, an imprint of the History Press, Stroud, Gloucestershire.

Leachman: "OC Desert", 1982, H V F Winstone, Quartet Books.

The Indian Army: The Garrison of British Imperial, 1974, T A Heathcote. Douglas David & Charles Ltd.

RAJ: The Making and Unmaking of British India, 1997, Lawrence James, Little, Brown Book Group.

Other books by Nigel Messenger.
www.nigelmessengerblog.wordpress.com

The Miracle of Michmash

Two battles, three thousand years apart yet almost identical in every detail. The British Army faced the Turks uphill towards Michmash with expected high loss of life when the proposed attack was due. A British major was reading the bible the night before the battle and found a reference to Michmash where the Israelites under Saul and his son, Jonathan, were facing a huge army of Philistines. Jonathan finds a secret passage enabling him to outflank the enemy. The major sends a group of men to find the passage and outflank the enemy in the same way as Jonathan did. History repeats itself after three thousand years. This was a mysterious and miraculous event which continues to confound historians.

The book follows the life and experiences of Jonathan and then fast-forwards to 1918 when the British Army is fighting the Turks in Palestine, following the adventures of chef and soldier, Bert Sugarman.

Andrews UK Ltd.

Megiddo, the Battles for Armageddon

Megiddo—the Armageddon of the Bible—three momentous battles took place near this ancient settlement in Palestine. Docker Nat Sullivan fights under General Allenby during the fierce allied campaign in WWI. He has vivid dreams about fighting with King Richard I in the Third Crusade and later for the Biblical Deborah, probably one of the greatest generals of all time. Nat returns to the docks and rises through the union ranks to become deputy to the political giant and statesman Ernest Bevan, General Secretary of the TUC. Nat, now a Labour MP, follows Ernest when he was appointed Minister of Labour during WW11 and later as his assistant when he was foreign secretary during the momentous post war years.

Three historic and portentous adventures helped shape the remarkable men of the twentieth century.

Andrews UK Ltd.